BUCHI EMECHETA was born in Lagos in Nigeria. Her father, a railway worker, died when she was very young. At the age of ten she won a scholarship to the Methodist Girls' High School, but by the time she was seventeen she had left school, married and had a child. She accompanied her husband to London where he was a student. Aged 22, she finally left him, and took an honours degree in sociology while supporting her five children and writing in the early morning.

Her first book, *In the Ditch*, details her experience as a poor, single parent in London. It was followed by *Second-Class Citizen*, *The Bride Price*, *The Slave Girl*, which was awarded the Jock Campbell Award, *The Joys Of Motherhood*, *Destination Biafra*, *Naira Power*, *Double Yoke*, *Gwendolen* and *The Rape of Shavi* as well as a number of children's books and two plays, *A Kind of Marriage*, produced on BBC television and *Juju Landlord*, produced by Granada. Her autobiography, *Head Above Water*, appeared in 1986 to much acclaim.

BUCHI EMECHETA

KEHINDE

Heinemann

Heinemann Educational Publishers
A Division of Heinemann Publishers (Oxford) Ltd
Halley Court, Jordan Hill, Oxford OX2 8EJ

Heinemann: A Division of Reed Publishing (USA) Inc.
361 Hanover Street, Portsmouth, NH 03801–3912, USA

Heinemann Educational Books (Nigeria) Ltd
PMB 5205, Ibadan
Heinemann Educational Boleswa
PO Box 10103, Village Post Office, Gaborone, Botswana

FLORENCE   PRAGUE   PARIS   MADRID
ATHENS   MELBOURNE   JOHANNESBURG
AUCKLAND   SINGAPORE   TOKYO
CHICAGO   SAO PAULO

First published by Heinemann Educational Publishers in 1994

Series Editor: Adewale Maja-Pearce

British Library Cataloguing in Publication Data
A catalogue record for this book is available from the British Library.

ISBN 0435 90985 1

Cover design by Touchpaper
Cover illustration by Synthia Saint James

Phototypeset by CentraCet Limited, Cambridge
Printed and bound in Great Britain
by Cox & Wyman Ltd, Reading, Berkshire

94 95 96 97   10 9 8 7 6 5 4 3 2

For Ijeoma Camilla
and
Chukwudi Adin

Acknowledgements

I wish to thank many friends for this book, *Kehinde*, but space will not allow.

My first thanks go to my best friends, 'Women of Pittsburgh, USA' – Brenda, Jackie, Familoni, Jane, etc. We spent hours debating about the so-called 'Black Women's Madness'.

I also wish to thank the Odozi Obodo Evangelical Church in Ibuza, Nigeria. They allowed me to watch closely how the prophets and prophetesses use the voices that come to them creatively.

And, last but not least, I wish to thank Jane Bryce in Barbados for editing the work at such short notice.

CONTENTS

1 The Letter

Albert picked up the letter. He gently lowered himself into the chair by the table. His hands were steady and controlled. On opening the letter, he laughed out loud. His family looked up, surprised, as Albert was a highly disciplined man who seldom allowed himself the luxury of loud natural laughter. Something omnious curled inside Kehinde's stomach. She had seen the back of the letter. It could come from only one source – Albert's sisters in Nigeria. Albert allowed himself a girlish giggle. His children, Bimpe and Joshua, stopped eating their tea. They looked at each other, shrugged and then smiled. Albert, who was not unaware of their impatience, prolonged and savoured the suspense.

'Who is it from?' asked Joshua, fourteen, scooping a spoon of baked beans into his mouth. He could not stand the exclusion any longer.

'It's a letter from Aunt Selina and Aunt Mary. They want me to return home.'

'They want you to return home? What of us?' Kehinde asked, bringing in a pot of tea. 'They have been hinting at it for a very long time, now they've got the courage to spell it out. Return home, return home indeed! They keep forgetting that you left Nigeria a young bachelor and that now you have a wife and kids. Return home, just like that, enh?'

'You know what home people are like. When they say "you", they mean all of us!' Albert explained in a voice so low and conciliatory that it was almost a whisper.

'Don't we count then?' Bimpe piped in.

1

'Will you keep quiet please, young lady! I happen to be talking to your mother.'

'She is right though,' Kehinde said as she sat down heavily in her kitchen chair, feeling suddenly tired and virtually useless. An eel of suspicion wriggled in the pit of her belly.

Theirs was a typical East London mid-terrace house with a small living room. Attached to the poky kitchen was a pantry, now converted into a dining room which was so small that when the family sat at their meal there was little room to move. There was another large room at the back, with a glass door opening into a small, untended garden. It was a room in which they could have eaten in comfort, a room the estate agent described as the morning room, but which the Okolos called the big bedroom. Kehinde and Albert slept there. What would they be doing with a morning room or a lounge, when they already had a living room in front and a pantry that served as a kitchen/diner? Their arrangement saved two bedrooms upstairs. They sublet one on a permanent basis, and the other one occasionally to bring in that extra pound or two. Whenever there were visitors from home they asked the temporary tenant, who was usually a student, to move.

Albert suspected that this was not the appropriate time to pursue the letter. He stuffed it into his shirt pocket, nonchalantly, putting on a big show for his watching family, to demonstrate that he did not care very much for what his sisters had to say. This had the desired effect. Kehinde sighed deeply and turned her attention from her husband to her kids.

Albert and Kehinde ate their ground rice and egusi soup. The children had recently started to complain about the monotony of having ground rice and soup every evening so once in a while, like tonight, to stem further argument, Kehinde would heat some baked beans and serve them on toast with a little salad of lettuce and tomatoes. The parents thought it was an awful meal, but the children knew what they wanted. They loved it, despite its plainness.

After satisfying herself that the family were tucking into their tea happily, Kehinde went on in a hurt tone. 'They did not even bother to ask how we are.' This was the right time to talk about her hurt at being regarded as a nonperson by her sister-in-law. 'All they know is come home, send money, come home. What is in Nigeria anyway? Are we not happy here? They just want a chance to nose into the way we live. Come home!'

'Well, they did ask how we all are. And they say there is an oil boom in Nigeria, and that one can actually pick work up in the streets. Nigeria needs us. The government says so. Even the Europeans are leaving their countries and rushing to Nigeria. My sisters are thinking of our own good, you know.'

'Leave the white people out of it. Everybody knows they always rush to any place that has cooked yams ready for them to eat.' Kehinde replied tightly in Igbo.

Joshua looked at his sister. 'Let's get out of here. Whenever they speak their language, it means they don't want us around.'

Kehinde, who was always indulgent towards her son, ignored his rudeness, which she rationalised as the normal behaviour of a fourteen-year-old boy establishing his identity. She simply laughed and ventured, 'Whose fault is it that you don't speak your mother tongue when you refuse to learn?'

'You mean *your* mother tongue. Mine is English. Remember you said that when I was born, the first thing you said to me was, "Hello Joshua!" So I speak the first language I heard.'

Kehinde started clearing away the tea things. Bimpe got up to help, squeezing in between chairs. Joshua, feeling left out, marched noisily out of the room, and soon after the sound of the television came through the wall.

It was Albert who noticed it was late and that the children were still watching television. It was always a battle to get them to go to bed; Joshua wanted to stay up and see the end of the football match, arguing that he was fourteen and all his friends at school would be talking about the match the next day. 'I'll look a fool, Dad, if I can't put in a word, just because you didn't let me stay up to watch. Think of it, Dad!'

Bimpe joined in, insisting that at eleven, she was practically a teenager too, and should not have to go to bed at nine o'clock, her agreed bed-time.

3

Albert swore under his breath, his face contorted in an effort to control himself. Both children were yelling like army sergeants. Albert walked deliberately to the television and switched it off. 'To bed, both of you. When I was your age, I didn't even have television. Off to bed.' The authoritative tone finally had an effect. Silence descended, and the two children slunk off to bed without saying good night.

Kehinde was already half asleep when Albert came into their bedroom. The quiet was a relief after the scene in the front room. 'Early to bed? It's only ten o'clock,' Albert commented, as he changed into his pyjamas.

'I keep telling you that I don't feel well. I haven't felt well for some time now. I was suspicious, so I went to the doctor this morning.'

'Suspicious of what?' Albert asked in a low and tremulous voice.

'I'm pregnant.'

'What? Pregnant? Kehinde, please sit up and look at me. What are you talking about?'

'I know how you must be feeling, especially now your sisters have suddenly realised they have a brother. Now you earn enough money, own a house . . .'

'*We* own a house,' Albert said quickly. He was not unaware of the legal status of a wife here in Britain. In Nigeria, the home belonged to the man, even if the woman spent her entire life keeping it in order. She could never ask her husband to leave the house, as was done here. But Albert did not want trouble, so for the sake of peace he said, 'Our house.'

In fact, Albert was only being realistic, since Kehinde earned more than he did. It was because of her position in the bank that they had been able to get a mortgage. But a good wife was not supposed to remind her husband of such things. When Kehinde said 'your house', she was playing the rôle of the 'good' Nigerian woman. Conversely, when he said 'our house', he was being careful not to upset her. After almost sixteen years of marriage, they played this game without thinking.

'I didn't get pregnant on purpose to thwart your going home

4

plans.' Kehinde wanted a real show down, but this time Albert refused to play.

'Going home plans? You make it sound as if I've been planning for it secretly.'

Albert, undressing in slow motion, regarded Kehinde as if she were an alien being, rather than the woman he'd lived with for fifteen years. Why become pregnant at this time of all times! He sat on the edge of the bed, his head bowed. Groping for comfort, he remembered how, when the children were little and they all slept in one room, they used to say their prayers together. When did they stop? He supposed the children must have grown out of it, and now he and Kehinde, despite their Catholic upbringing, no longer prayed either. Evidently conversion had not been able to eradicate their parents' long-held traditional beliefs. They both came from polygamous families – his father had two wives, Kehinde's three. The Irish priests, not knowing which way to turn, had baptized them all, seeing it as a chance to save these 'lost souls' for Christ. Abruptly, Albert's thought returned to the present.

'How did it happen? I thought I'd been careful,' he asked aloud.

'How am I to know, enh? I always warn you not to bother me when I'm asleep. Haven't I been warning you that it could happen? When you wanted to come inside me earlier on in our marriage, you used to be so nice. You took the trouble to wake me up with love. Now you're always impatient. You grip my breasts from behind as if you're going to force yourself on me, and before I know what you're about, you're done. I don't even know if you're using any protection or not. So I hope you're not doing like some Nigerian men and suggesting it's *my* fault.'

Albert ignored her complaint about his sexual methods, but was curious to find out what she meant by her reference to Nigerian men.

'Are you the only one who doesn't know about the latest method of blackmailing women into submissiveness?' she retorted. 'They say: "You are not carrying my child," and the woman ends up spending time and money to prove that the child really *is* his.'

Albert chuckled in spite of himself. Yes, he knew of a few instances. A tough woman could be brought to heel by a husband claiming that the child she was carrying was not his, and then forgiving her all the same. She would never be able to hold up her head among his people. Very few would believe the woman's side of the story, and a woman who dared to suggest a blood test to clear her name was considered presumptuous. Yes, a neat blackmail.

Albert turned off the bedside lamp and sat in the dark, considering. He had already made the decision to return home. It was only a matter of when. After eighteen years, he pined for sunshine, freedom, easy friendship, warmth. If he could get Kehinde on his side, winning the children over would be easy. He wanted to go home and show off his new life-style, his material success. He would be able to build houses, to be someone. Nigeria was booming, and he wanted to join the party. Now this hiccough. What to do, enh?

Albert was a thin, wiry man of forty. Kehinde, who had never been thin, was now, at thirty-five and after the births of two children and years of eating takeaway fish and chips, comfortably plump. Albert liked her that way. He found thin women unsatisfying. What was a man expected to fondle at night, when there was a gale outside? Give him a plump African woman with a heavy backside, like Kehinde. He looked in her direction. 'What are we going to do, enh?'

'You asking me what you are going to do? Are you no longer the head of the family? Bimpe is almost twelve after all. She is not too young to have a brother or sister, or is she?' Kehinde was aware that she could talk to her husband less formally than women like her sister, Ifeyinwa, who were in more traditional marriages. She related to Albert as a friend, a compatriot, a confidant. This was one of the reasons for the uneasiness she had felt earlier that evening, when Albert was reading the letter from home.

Albert's heart sank. 'Kehinde, what of your promotion? And

6

we've only just recovered from the last lot of child minders.' Kehinde was intransigent.

'So, what do you want me to do? Our people believe that people are more valuable than money.'

'I know all that. But our people never lived in London, where parents have to pay a great part of their wages to nannies to look after their babies.'

Kehinde sucked her teeth and turned her face to the wall, pulling the bed clothes to her side. Giving up, Albert got into bed. He did not complain about the bed clothes. It was too late for an altercation, but he lay rigid for a long time. He had planned to calm her about the letter by making love to her in that particular way she favoured. He would have stroked her legs, working his hands up gradually until his fingers were inside her body. With his other hand, he would have played *koto* with her nipples. Her breasts were warm, full and cushiony. She would have gasped and the night play would have begun. And then, while carried away, she would have agreed that going home was not only a good idea, but the best and only plan for them.

But the news of the pregnancy had spoilt all that. A police siren tore into his thoughts, and set him wondering whether it was right to drive at such high speed. They could end up killing an innocent somebody. He turned this way and that way, wondering about it.

2   Kehinde and Moriammo

Despite the sunshine, there was a chill in the air, causing Kehinde and her friend to pull their Marks and Spencers raincoats closer to their bodies.

'This new bank building is overheated, *abi*?' Kehinde observed.

'It's better than being cold,' Moriammo responded.

'I'm not complaining.' The two women, who worked together in the bank in Crouch End, walked briskly to the local Wimpy bar, just a block away. They ordered beef burgers and coffee.

'Can you count the number of times we've been here over the past ten years or so?' Moriammo asked idly, biting into her food. They had to eat quickly as it was Friday, and they had to dash and do the shopping during their lunch break. Kehinde did not feel like hurrying. She was taking tiny sips of coffee.

Moriammo watched her for a while and said with her mouth full, 'Eh, today na Friday. We get plenty shopping to do. Why you dey chop small, small, like *oyinbo*?'

'Not be only *oyinbos* wey chop small small. In fact, sef, dem chop so so fast too. You never see those women wey dey sell cabbage for market chop?'

They both laughed, but the laughter stopped abruptly, as if on cue.

Moriammo, with her dark brown eyes that were always edged with black *tiro*, peered closely at Kehinde.

'What is the matter? *Abi*, you done quarrel with Alby?'

'Oh, I no know, Moriammo. I don tell am say, I pregnant.'

'Hm, him no happy? These our men just wan make we get belle every time.'

8

'I beg stop-o, Moriammo. Your voice dey give me headache!'

Moriammo became thoughtful, chewing slowly and not saying anything for a while. Kehinde had been snappy all morning, whereas Kehinde and Albert should be happy that there was going to be another baby. After all, Bimpe was almost twelve now.

Kehinde pushed her beef burger away and said, 'Sorry-o, Moriammo. Only say, sometimes I no understand that man I marry. He dey worry more for my job here for bank than for the pikin. And to make matters worse, him sisters write from home say make we return. Dem say money plenty for Lagos, and jobs dey go for two for half a penny.'

'Well, dat no be bad thing, *abi*? I wan go home too. My trouble be say Tunde no get qualification at all at all. Dat man, him no get no experience in anything except to write ticket for Nigeria Airways counter.'

They laughed again.

'Him be good man, though. They fit transfer him to home branch, you know Moriammo. Dem say our Naira almost be the same as pound. The value just dey rise every day.'

'I know, I dey see am every day for the exchange rate table. But why you and Alby careless so, 'specially as he no sure if him want any more pikin? Shame on you both. Dis na England, abi you done forget? Here two pickin dey fine.'

'Boh, go siddown my friend. You wan tell me say you and Tunde no dey do the tin for night again? Go siddown, boh. Who you dey deceive? Me? Wetin worry me be my promotion here.' The smile had disappeared from Kehinde's face. 'If I born this pikin, I go take almost one year off work. Boh, all this *wahala*!'

'Na wa-o. After all the *wahala* wey you go through before dem 'gree promise to give you promotion. This trouble, na wa! We women no dey win anyting for this world! I tink say Alby right to worry about it though. But, hmm, you go get the promotion. I dey sure.'

'Where I go get the promotion, enh? Where? Here or for Nigeria? *Abi*, you done deaf now? I tell you say, Albert's sisters write say make we come home.'

'So, wetin you wan do? Tanda here when Alby stay at home? You go let him stay home alone among those Nigerian acadas? You no know say those young overeducated women dey thirst for been-to men as small baby dey thirst for suck? I no dey-o! Make you think twice, my friend.'

'My Alby no be like that. Him different. I fit swear with my life for him,' Kehinde defended her husband. And she felt she was speaking the truth, since Albert had never given her cause to worry about unfaithfulness.

'Kehinde, I beg, wake up-o; make you just wake up.'

'Wetin you mean Moriammo? I tell you say Alby no be like that.'

Their attention was diverted by the entrance of two young women with six young children between them. The children looked pinched and deprived, the mothers harassed. It was not the first time Kehinde and Moriammo had seen them.

'These ones na one-parent family. Homeless, too,' Moriammo commented.

'Ah, how you know that? They just be ordinary women with unemployed husbands.'

Moriammo shook her head. 'No, I heard them talk the other day. Dem dey lie for that bed and breakfast place up Crouch Hill. Allah! I no understand why some women fit allow themselves to be trapped in such a situation. Why dem no get jobs, even if na ordinary cleaning?'

A thoughtful pause followed, during which the two black women, well established in their jobs and in their homes, scrutinised the two younger women.

'And dis be dem country too. I think they just lazy,' whispered Moriammo, who could only see that the women were white. 'You know Tunde's cousin, Abeke, she dey read to be sociologist. She don tell me say some of these women just get pikin, so the government go give them flat. Look that one, wetin she won do with three pikin when she self still be one?'

'Well this story done get K-leg, as we say for Eko. Boh my sister, make we dey go, we get shopping to do,' said Kehinde. 'I

10

didn't touch this food. I wonder, would they be offended if I gave it to them?'

Moriammo shrugged her shoulders. She put on her coat and patted her hair into place, making sure she did not look at the young women and their families. 'Make you try, now. They fit only say no. Women like them, no dey have racial prejudice. They can't afford it.'

Kehinde got up. With unsure steps she walked to the older of the two women. She whispered, 'I ordered food, but I haven't touched it. I don't feel hungry, I'm expecting a baby you see, still very early. I'm going through the sickness stage.'

'Are yer? I know all about it. Ta very much. Jodiiiii, bring that plate over. The lady gave it to us.'

'The beef burgers and all? Corrr!' cried five-year-old Jodi, as he dashed towards the table at which Kehinde and Moriammo had been eating. He was so unabashed that everybody laughed.

'You done do your Christian act for the day,' commented Moriammo, as they walked away. 'Poor kid. Must be hard though, raising kids in this town with no husband.' The child's naturalness had apparently touched her heart.

'Yes, and no home. Well, we work hard for wh..t we have. I don't have much sympathy for them. Some women choose a life like that to prove how tough they can be.'

'Come on, Kehinde, no sane woman go choose such a life. Na just by mistake or hard luck. Not everybody get good luck for this world, you know.'

'I tell you, I have seen one such woman. She's a townwoman of ours. She has six kids. She said her husband beat her, so she left him. Of course the man disappeared. The woman now lives in a council flat – one of those dangerous and filthy ones. What annoys Alby is that she noises any little success she has, as if we all cared. The other day, she gave a party because she had bought a sewing machine. Imagine!'

Moriammo laughed. 'Well, oyibos do that too. I've seen it in *Fiddler on the Roof.* The young couple invited the whole village because they had bought a new sewing machine. They called it a new arrival.'

11

'O Moriammo, be serious. Alby no dey allow me to associate with such women. We no get anyting in common!'

'But dat woman get heart-o. Six pikin! Allah *Baba*!'

'And she is so well educated too. She should have known better.'

'Maybe too much book bad for women. Tunde don dey say so often. If she no be so much acada, she for don stay for her children at least. Now the husband dey enjoy. And when the children don grow finish, them go forgive them papa. Allah, please lend a hand to the women of the world.'

'Exactly, that's what I been dey say. Monkey dey work, baboon dey chop.'

'Wetin be im name self, this your townswoman? Just curious.'

'Her name na Mrs Elikwu – Mary Elikwu,' Kehinde spat.

'Allah, lend a hand. Una women too stubborn, self. Six pikin, no be joke-o.'

By the door, Moriammo laid a hand on Kehinde's shoulder and confided in a low tone. 'You know I go try make another child. You never know, maybe I get lucky and have a man-child this time after my two girls.'

'Moriammo, you be copy cat.'

'I know. Better than being jealous.'

'You tink say Tunde go gree?'

'I go make am gree. By force!'

They laughed helplessly as they crossed the road and entered the big supermarket in front of the clock tower. Moriammo took two wire baskets from the stack by the automatic doors and gave one to Kehinde.

'Thank you, my friend.'

'Any time,' said Moriammo, in a voice like a song.

12

3 Albert's Workplace

One of the reasons Albert Okolo chose to live in Leytonstone was because of its nearness to his workplace. He had only to drive for about fifteen minutes and he would be there. He could virtually slip out of the house a few minutes before his work started without disturbing his family.

He never ate breakfast, a habit he had from Nigeria. He slid out of bed not wanting to disturb Kehinde and drove to work mechanically. He had driven that same road, that same corner and that short-cut, so often that he could do the distance with his eyes closed. At work, he slipped mechanically into the routine of his job as storekeeper.

'Morning Alby,' greeted his colleague, Mike Levy.

'Morning Mike,' Albert drawled. He did not have to look up; he knew who it was. For once, he did not go on to ask about Mike's health and that of his family, a Nigerian habit Albert had never shaken off, even after eighteen years. It was so automatic that Mike waited unconsciously for it and unwittingly readied himself with the usual answer: 'They are well, at least they were when I left home.' And Albert would say in reply, 'That's all right. We thank God for another day.' The omission alerted Mike that something was wrong. He watched his colleague thoughtfully.

Others came in, who, in the English manner, did not bother to say 'Good morning', except for Prahbu, a man they called 'India' even though he came from Pakistan, who greeted all the other storekeepers and went straight to the tea machine. The noise of

13

his ten pence pieces rattled Albert and he lifted his dark lean face to look at Prahbu.

'Heh, what's the matter with 'im?' Prahbu asked Mike.

'How should I know? Why don't you ask him? He's your friend too.'

They all set to work in the cluttered warehouse, checking, labelling, dusting, checking again and stamping. Albert had to examine and enter the figures and pass them to the gov'nor, who had a separate box-like room.

'I'm buying tea for everybody today,' Prahbu announced at the mid-morning break.

'Is it your birthday then?' asked John, one of the English workers, now fully awake and friendlier.

'Nope, I just feel like buying tea for everybody,' Prahbu said in the sing song voice he sometimes affected for fun.

'I didn't know that Hindus drank tea. You're the first I've seen.' John was at his jokes again.

'I am not a Hindu, you know that,' Prahbu said, laughing. John had always said this since he had realised it annoyed Prahbu at the beginning of their association. Not only that, but John soon realised that calling him 'India' was even more annoying. Prahbu, however, soon got wise, and learnt to react with humour, which took the sting out of John's spite.

'What does it matter what religion? God did not forbid tea. What does your God say, Albert? You're a Catholic, aren't you?' Prahbu turned the banter on Albert, who was far too quiet this morning.

'Yes, I'm a Catholic and I'm about to commit a mortal sin,' he responded.

John spilled his tea. 'Wharr? Are you going to kill us for voodoo?' Albert looked at John and suddenly noticed that the slim Cockney who had joined them over ten years before was getting portlier and portlier, while his high forehead was graduating into baldness. He still had his tiny pink mouth which had the unexpected habit of breaking into laughter when everybody else had finished laughing.

Albert remained silent. He had to talk to Prahbu privately.

14

Prahbu was his closest mate. John took out his plastic darts and threw them at the picture of a woman in a bikini pinned to the wall.

At their lunch break, Prahbu sat next to Albert.

'Now, my friend, what's the problem?'

'Kehinde is pregnant.'

'Oh? So what is the problem?'

Albert thought carefully before he replied. He knew the advice he wanted from his colleague, just as he had wanted Mike to approve of his circumcising his son Joshua, years ago.

'She's going to be made a branch manager soon. Can you imagine what will happen to her promotion if they realise she's going on maternity leave?'

'Shsh,' Prahbu whispered, making a downward movement with his hand. 'They will demote her, or tell her to go back home and have as many children as she wants. Hm, such jobs are not easy to find these days, 'specially for our people. Your wife is very, very lucky to have that job.'

'Yes, I know. That's exactly what I mean. I can't imagine her walking into another job like that these days.'

'But you have two kids already, so why not this one?'

Albert shrugged. 'This is not the right time for another one. I know abortion is wrong but we are in a strange land, where you do things contrary to your culture.'

'Was that what you had in mind? Abortion?'

Albert nodded.

'What does your wife say to that? Our women can be difficult when it comes to things like that. A white woman, easy, she'll see sense.'

'Er . . . I haven't even told her yet. But she will do what I say, after a lot of tantrums. Stupid country, where you need your wife's money to make ends meet.'

'I know what you mean. Women rule in this country,' Prahbu said in a long-suffering voice. 'And children are regarded as a luxury.'

Albert nodded. 'In my country, children are a necessity. They

15

mean a good old age with plenty to eat. And with grandchildren, people respect you.'

'Now you're telling me. You know I have three boys, but Leila must not get pregnant again until I can join her full-time in our shop.'

'How is that going?' Albert asked, putting some life into his voice for the first time that day. He was always interested in Prahbu's business projects.

Prahbu undulated his right hand, enjoying the attention Albert was giving him. 'So . . . so. Rome was not built in a day.'

They all had their dreams. Prahbu's was to own big grocery stores and newsagent's shops. Mike dealt in stocks and shares and had many contacts through his synagogue. John and the others dreamt of holiday villas in Spain or Madeira, where they could live in retirement. Albert's dream was to be made a chief in his homeland, but while the others could talk about their dreams, Albert felt shy. He was afraid Prahbu would ask, 'Are you sure you're doing the right thing, going back to Africa?' Albert knew that their images of African chiefs were gathered from old Tarzan films and *Sanders of the River*, and that trying to give his colleagues an up-to-date picture of Nigeria would be a waste of time.

Today Albert did not indulge himself with dreams. He was too preoccupied by Kehinde's announcement of the night before. He did not even tell Prahbu about the letter he had received from home the day before. Instead, he continued the conversation they had started.

'You will make it, Prahbu. Your people are very hard working.'

'So are your people, my friend,' Prahbu said generously. He did not indulge in the usual stories of his newspaper distribution work. He could see that today Albert needed a listening ear, and a pat on the back.

'Hmm, but your people are born businessmen,' Albert said.

'Ha, ha, ha, what of Nigerians!'

'You're too kind Prahbu.'

'Good luck, my friend.'

16

4 Kehinde and Albert

It was a mild spring evening, crisp and windy, but not cold. It
was nearly seven and the rush-hour was over as they cruised
slowly, Albert searching the house-fronts for the clinic address.
Hugging the kerb, they approached a lone woman in a red
leather mini-skirt and a cheap fur coat. Her steps slowed as they
drew level and she bent down to look inside the car. Seeing
Kehinde, she straightened abruptly and wiggled away, a wraith-
like worm of cigarette smoke trailing behind her.

Kehinde, hunched miserably in her seat, thought that, after
all, Albert had brought her to the level of that woman – that
prostitute. To him, they were the same, just bodies, convenient
vehicles which, when they took on an inconvenient burden, could
be emptied of it by the same means. Into Kehinde's mind,
interrupting her thoughts, came a voice, the same voice she often
heard when she was lonely or confused. 'Our mother died having
you. I too died so you could live. Are you now going to kill your
child before he has a chance of life?'

Taiwo: the one who preceded me into the world. There were two
of us in our mother's womb. We had no will of our own. We
followed the rhythm of everything around us. Our food came
from mother, and in return, we passed our waste back into our
mother's blood. Soon we started running short of the water of
life. Everything was becoming short and cramped. At length, we
started to talk to each other, sharing as best we could for survival,
becoming weaker and weaker by the day together. Nonetheless,

17

we managed to survive for months, touching and kissing, making the best of the space available. Together we fought against the skin that kept us captive. We wanted to burst out and escape into the open. We did not know what lay out there in the world, but anything, anywhere was better than where we were. We communicated with each other by touch and by sounds. Sounds which only we could understand. Then one day, we laid siege on the skin wall that kept us enclosed. Frustrated, we banged and we shouted; and we kicked and cried in our limited space. Exhausted, I fell asleep. I felt even in sleep the cessation of the rhythmical movements I was accustomed to. I felt around me in the now warm thickening water for my sister, but she had become just a lump of lifeless flesh. I clung to her, because she had been the only living warmth I knew. I called her, but there was no answer. I cried for her in my now lonely tomb. None heard my cries. I hugged her, held her to myself, so tightly that the wetness from her body started flowing into mine. As she dried, I had more space. I grew bigger. I survived. But I did not eat my sister, as they said I did. There was only life enough for one of us.

Our mother, poor soul, must have gone through hell giving birth to us. Yes, I wanted to come out first. To be the Taiwo, the one who tasted the world first. I tried to hold back what was left of my sister, but even her wrinkled lifeless flesh had a strong stubborn will. Her tiny wizened head came out first. My mother had no more energy to give birth to me, who by this time was so big, like two babies in one. They cut her open and I, Kehinde, the twin who follows behind, was taken out. My mother and my sister were dead. Nobody wanted me. Luckily, Aunt Nnebogo came to visit, and she took me away from all those people who accused me of being a child who brought bad luck. But Aunt Nnebogo took the risk, and it paid her. She took me away to where she lived, in far-off Lagos, where the Yoruba people believe that twins bring luck, and give them special names: Taiwo and Kehinde. They say that as soon as I came into Aunt Nnebogo's life, her fish business flourished. She had enough money to rent a room of her own in Macaullum Street in Ebute

Metta. She became independent, and was rich enough to be able to afford the burial of her mother who died when she was quite little.

Nobody told me that Aunt Nnebogo was not my mother, and that was what I called her till I was eleven years old. When they gave me *akara* or *moyin-moyin* as a toddler, I would share it into two, part for me and part for my Taiwo – the one who came to taste life for me. I did this even though I did not know I was a twin, or that I had deprived my Taiwo of her life. I even talked to her in my sleep, without knowing who I was talking to. Sometimes Aunt Nnebogo used to be impatient and angry over my wanting to do everything twice. I later realized that she did not want me to know the story of my birth. She knew people would remember and say, 'Was this not that baby that brought bad luck to her mother and baby sister? Was this not the child that deprived her brothers and sisters of the joy of having a mother? What are you doing with such an ill-luck child?' But Aunt Nnebogo had no child of her own, and she wanted to protect me. She even gave me a Christian name: Jacobina, after Jacob, who fought and won the battle against his brother Esau in the Bible. Aunt Nnebogo loved the Bible stories, which reminded her of our moonlight stories. She told me that story so many times that, for a while, I thought it was the story of my own birth.

I think I was about five or so when we saw an *iyabeji* – the name the Yorubas give to the mother of twins – dancing as those mothers do. She came with her twins in front of the fish stall where my Aunt sold fish. I was at the back of the stall, sitting on a mat with my feet wide apart, enjoying the coolness of the beaten earth. I was eating *iwu-akpu*, which I liked because it was cool and filling and really tasty. I was, as usual, leaving a handful in this corner for my *chi* and in that corner for my Taiwo. I was cheating because I liked *iwu-akpu* a lot, so I was telling Taiwo, 'You have this little bit, but I am going to eat this big bit because I am very hungry.'

The *iyabeji* came with her *onilu* and started to sing the praises of her twins, informing us that 'the twins' mother is saying hello

19

to you all.' Her voice was haunting and poignant, and everybody was drawn in:

'Iyabeji nki yio . . .
Eru o be mio lati bi 'be ji o . . .'

She went on to sing of how she was not afraid to be the mother of twins, to list the twins' attributes and to pray for the good will of all present.

I stopped eating. The *onilu* drummed hard, and the *iyabeji* danced low, bending her knees and moving in beautiful rhythm to the song and the drum. The haunting melody of the *ibeji* song mesmerised the fish-stall holders. The twins, one in front and the other on the mother's back, peeped out at the people with the wide eyes of innocence. My eyes caught theirs and held for a split second.

Something inside me burst, like the rupturing of a boil. An old question that had been festering for a long time was answered at that moment.

I scrambled up, upsetting my bowl of *iwu-akpu*, and dashed to Aunt Nnebogo. 'Where is my Taiwo – the person who tasted the world for me?' I cried. My voice, high and hysterical, drowned that of the *iyabeji*. 'We were two, weren't we?' I insisted, with the certainty of revelation.

Iyabeji stopped dancing. All eyes were diverted from her to rest on me. The *iyabeji* drummer smiled and asked, 'So the little girl is a twin?' Aunt Nnebogo had to nod. She was scared out of her wits at the scene I was making and did not have time to think of the right answer. She just nodded, like a shocked lizard after it has fallen from a tree. I was only quiet when everybody in the fish stalls contributed money, fish and little gifts and asked me to carry them to the twins. I loved that, being chosen to give two sets of gifts to the mother of twins, to give to twins like me.

When the *iyabeji* left, everybody started to ask where my Taiwo was, and why it was that a replica of my lost sister had not been made for me to carry. Mama Comfort, the stallholder next to us, who was also from our part of Nigeria, kept asking Aunt Nnebogo, 'When did you have a set of twins? You know you should be called by the twins' names, otherwise they may become bad luck. So you're "twins'-mother" then.'

My aunt shook her head at the curious women, putting her finger to her lips. She made frantic signs to silence them in my presence. I was not too young to be aware of this. I knew even then that she was going to give them an explanation. But what Mama Comfort said next rang in my mind long after: 'I always thought when she divided her food in two before eating that she was giving it to her *chi*.' Aunt Nnebogo replied in a low tone, 'Her second and her *chi* are one and the same.'

When we got home from the market that day, I became ill. People made suggestions as to the cause of my fever. But Aunt Nnebogo was a Christian. When she had snatched me away from the negative situation in which I was born, she had thought she was saving me from the clutches of superstition. She did not know that I would grow into a child who would not let her identity die. I kept asking, 'Where is my sister? Where is my Taiwo?' I knew that my second was a girl, just as nobody had to tell me that I was born one of a set of twins.

Some people who knew had made hints in unguarded moments about my past, because they felt my birth caused a disaster, and those hints must have entered my subconscious. I called Aunt Nnebogo 'Mama', because she was the only mother I knew. Other people called her Mama Jacobina, and she answered to it, but I always sensed that she did not allow the milk of her love to flow unchecked as many mothers around me did. Most mothers gave too much love and tried to own the beloved. But I was haunted by my past, so that Aunt Nnebogo put me on the hem of the skirt of her love. However, for me to get fully well, she asked a special *ibeji* carver to make me my Taiwo. They must have told her to start calling me my real name, Kehinde, and within a few years, I had forgotten that I had been called another name.

Back to present

Kehinde was recalled to the present by Albert's voice. Tentatively he said, 'I'm sorry we have to do this. When we get home to Nigeria, you can have as many babies as you like, I promise.'

21

angered

Kehinde flared up instantly. 'What do you mean, have as many babies as I like? Have you forgotten that they are tying my tubes as well? I meant what I said last night. If I abort this child, I want my tubes tied. I can no longer rely on you to take the proper precautions. And I don't want to go through this again, ever.'

Albert threw a worried look at her, rubbing tears of anger and frustration from her eyes. He did not care for this tube-tying business, but Kehinde had made it a condition for the abortion. He had had to agree. There was no way he could save for their home-going on his income alone, to say nothing of feeding another mouth. He consoled himself that if doctors could tie up women's tubes, surely they could untie them again whenever he and Kehinde could afford another child.

'When we get to Nigeria,' Kehinde continued, 'if I am really going with you, I am going to enjoy myself. I'm not going to get there and start carrying babies again. If I can't have this one here, then I'm not having any there. And I may not even go with you. My dreams about home are confused. I haven't a clear vision what I'm supposed to be looking for there. So hurry up and tell your . . . sisters whatever you like.'

Kehinde had been tempted to call his sisters a bad name, but she dared not. The Igbo woman in her knew how far to go. She could tell Albert what she liked, but would not malign his relatives. Not to his face, at any rate.

Albert ignored her, attributing her peevishness to nervousness about the operation.

'Ah, here we are, number 71,' he said with relief, drawing up at the front door of the clinic.

Kehinde's heart beat fast, like hailstones on a tin roof. She felt she was making a momentous decision, and her legs were like jelly, scarcely able to carry her weight. Had Albert said at that juncture, 'Let's go back home darling. Our dreams should be locked in each other's fate, not mine and yours separate,' she might have loved him devotedly for the rest of her life. But he did not. She walked like a zombie to the front door. Albert must have rung the bell.

doesn't want to do this.

22

A woman in a white uniform, wearing a strictly commercial smile, looked them up and down.

'Come in, Mrs Okolo. Your room is ready for you. Come on in.'

The hallway was high and huge. The floor was beautifully tiled and there was a big crystal chandelier hanging from the ceiling. On the right, a wood and iron stairway curved itself snake-like to the floor above. On the left was a table so highly polished that it could have been made of glass. The vase of yellow roses it held was reflected in its surface. The atmosphere spelt money. Kehinde thought of how much they were paying.

'Think how much it costs to raise a child these days,' Albert had said only the night before, and she had agreed they could not afford another one. But they could afford this. ~ ironic

She was propelled into a room, clinically clean, with two single beds, lush green carpet on the floor, and a bedside table with crab-like legs. There was a television with video paraphernalia against the window, so elaborately draped it looked like a stage set. There was no one in the other bed, for which Kehinde gave thanks.

'I'll be back tomorrow to take you home, around this time. Isn't that so, nurse?' Albert, having come this far with her, was in a hurry to be gone. The woman with the commercial smile caught Albert's eye and nodded. 'Yes, around this time tomorrow. It will be done first thing in the morning, but we like our mothers . . . our patients to have a few hours rest before leaving. So you're quite right, Mr Okolo.'

'I *am* a mother. A mother of two,' Kehinde snapped illogically at the poor woman.

Albert and the nurse jumped. The nurse recovered first.

'Oh,' her expensive smile creased the corners of her mouth, revealing almost the complete set of pearly teeth. 'Oh, so I am not wrong then in calling you a mother.'

'And this is my husband,' Kehinde wanted to add. 'I am not a whore, beating the street. I am a respectable woman.' But her shaking body stopped her. She sat down untidily on the tidily made bed.

'Goodbye Mr Okolo, we'll see you tomorrow.'

Albert bent down and gave her a moist kiss on the cheek. Kehinde felt it was a show for the watching nurse. Kissing, after all, was not part of their culture.

'Goodbye, K-k, I'll see you tomorrow.' Albert threw a parting glance in her direction, then he walked briskly out of the door.

I am not going to cry, stupid woman. Two children are enough. I don't care if my mother already had eight children when she died having me and my twin sister, Taiwo – the one who tasted the world for me. The one who died with Mother. I am not paying any mind to all that. Not at all.

5   *Another Patient*

She must have slept, which surprised her. She would have
thought that the beating of her heart would make sleep imposs-
ible. When she opened her eyes, she was facing the wall, but was
conscious of the sound of someone sniffing.

A figure was lying on the other bed, her brown hair tumbled
all over the single pillow. She was small and looked young, much
younger than Kehinde. Kehinde propped her head on her elbow
and watched the girl's shoulders convulsed in spasmodic sobs.
Eventually, when she could bear it no longer, she put her own
guilt and uncertainty to the back of her mind, and said, 'Don't
worry. It will all be over in the morning.'

The convulsions slowed, degenerating into hiccoughs and
sniffing. Kehinde lay down and tried to flip through one of the
glossy magazines on the bedside table. She watched the girl at
the same time. At last the girl turned, and Kehinde saw her face,
the face of a confused child. White people's faces look red when
they cry, but hers was dead white and flat like pizza dough, with
red blotches like tomato purée. Without make-up, some faces are
almost too rude to be shown in public, like a nude adult going to
market.

'I must apologise, I just can't help myself.' She had an
educated voice. Though she was young, there was no doubt that
she was in control as soon as she opened her mouth. She made it
clear that she had just indulged herself a little by crying. 'With
all the money my boyfriend had to pay, at least they should have
given me a private room. But then we probably have to pay for
the superior location and the quality furniture.'

'That's all right.' Kehinde, too, started to use her assistant bank manager voice. 'I was doing some soul-searching earlier on, but must have drifted off to sleep. My nerves have been taut the past weeks. Now that I'm here, I feel almost relaxed and at peace. As if it's all out of my hands.'

The girl said nothing, just looked. Kehinde did not mind doing the talking. She wanted to talk, talking was like a prayer.

'I have to go through with it. My husband will kill me if I don't. But really, inside, I'm confused. Part of me doesn't want any more children, another part wants to keep this one, just this one. I think it's because I was born one of twins I always have to weigh things this way and that before I make a decision. Can you understand that?'

The girl nodded. Kehinde was surprised at herself, confiding in a strange girl, almost ten years her junior. She came from a culture in which being older meant being wiser, commanding respect. This girl should have been crying on her shoulder, and instead, Kehinde herself was talking shamelessly. The girl just sniffed.

'My husband and I are going back home, back to Nigeria. That's why we don't want the baby. We have a year or so left here, so I need to work hard to save more money.'

The girl sat up gently. She arranged her pillow so that Kehinde could see her more clearly. Her eyes were red rimmed, as if she'd been crying for days. She gently pushed her brown hair away from her face. Every gesture she made was slow and calculated. Furrowing her brows, she peered at Kehinde, who felt more guilty than ever. But she could not stop herself. 'We have been here eighteen years, you see. My husband is the first son, and even though we've been here all this time, we still have to go home. So we don't want this child. That's why I'm here.'

The girl lay back on the bed as if she was going to start sobbing again. Kehinde felt like crying out, 'Say something to me. I don't care if you're white or young enough to be my younger half-sister. Just say something to me.' She took a good hold of herself and asked aloud, 'Are you all right?'

26

The girl nodded, arranging the bed clothes over herself, and did not cry.

The nurse's footsteps padded on the corridor. She came in and asked, 'All right, ladies?' in a sugary voice. The plastic smile was unwavering, but she was looking tired. Kehinde could see a faint line on her brow, and wondered how old she was. She left them each with a nightcap.

'Makes sleep so much easier,' she said brightly, to no one in particular. She was obviously used to patients not responding to her empty, honeyed words. Taking out something that looked like a tiny calculator from her apron pocket, she pointed it at the window and pressed. The curtains swished closed. Kehinde's mouth opened when she saw the miracle the little calculator could perform. If her room-mate was surprised, she did not show it. 'Good night ladies,' the nurse intoned, as she padded out of the room.

Kehinde turned off her bedside lamp, pulled the sheets up to her chin and said, 'Good night.' Then she added, 'They call me Kehinde. I don't know your name.'

A long silence followed, broken eventually by the girl's tight little voice.

'Goodnight, Kehinde. Thank you for talking to me. My name is Leah. I want my baby badly, but I can't afford to keep it. I have no home, I have no job, I've dropped out of university, and I'm not even sure I love David. I don't want to trap him. That would be unfair.'

It was Kehinde's turn to be silent.

'What makes me angry is this. Why am I feeling so sad about it all?' Leah's voice was a cry from the heart.

Kehinde wanted to say so many things, but Leah had turned off her light. Words were unnecessary anyhow, as the nightcap was taking effect. God only knew what the nurse with honeyed words had put in it. Whatever it was, it succeeded in making Kehinde's mouth unable to say what her heart was thinking.

6   The Dream

'It won't be much, Mrs Okolo, just a prick and you won't feel a thing.' Feeling . . . fear, clutching my heart. Swooning, noises in my ears. Children's voices as we play in the street, under the eyes of the bread, groundnut and sugarcane sellers from the yard, displaying their wares on the pavement. We are playing a game of families. Olu is refusing to play mother, because her mother has died, gone away, neglecting Olu and her brother Akintunde. Each time we remember, we are silent with sorrow.

'No, no, Malechi,' the big girl from next door is saying. 'Olu has no mother, so she can play father.'

'Why would she play father, when she's not a boy?' I ask angrily.

'Because. This is a play family, not a real one. And in real life, she has no mother,' Elofune, Malechi's sister, defends Olu, and everyone glares at me.

'Well, what am I going to play then? Can I play mother?'

They all laugh, pointing at me. 'Just because you have no father, you think a family must always have a mother. But there are many mothers in a compound, so you can have a family without a particular mother.'

'Yes, but some families have no father, too,' I say in my stubborn way, my anger rising as I remember that I still do not know who my real mother is. 'All right, all right,' says Malechi, wondering what this circular argument is all about. 'You, Kehinde, play mother, because you have no father and Olu, you play father as you have no mother.'

As usual I will not let the matter rest. I want to go on arguing,

28

flash-back

as if the more I argue, the more likely the enigma of my birth will be explained to me. My mind is not on the game. Olu's mother died. Where is my father, did he die too? I look at the adults, but they are talking amongst themselves. I am left with a familiar feeling of helplessness.

The moon goes behind a cloud, and the fire flies become more audacious. The Hausas who live down the road and buy food from us until late at night have all bought their food. We are tired of playing, and are now telling stories, but our songs are dying in our throats. The night wind is cold, after the airless heat of the day. Those awake enough to answer the call songs of the stories are answering them half-heartedly. We are beginning to fall asleep. Aunt Nnebogo calls in her low voice, 'Kehinde, don't fall asleep yet. Take the unsold groundnuts inside and then go to the backyard and pee before you go in.'

'Yes Mama,' I reply. I do not get up immediately because our room is at the back of the house. To get there we have to pass the room of the landlord and his people, and walk along a dark corridor, with no electric light.

'Are you coming?' I ask sleepily.

'Why? Are you frightened of the dark? Only witches are frightened of the dark.'

The statement shocks me into wakefulness. Other parents drag or carry their children inside at night. I want Aunt Nnebogo to do the same, as if she were really my mother. I want to show that I'm like the other children in the yard.

Inside our room, darkness wells around us like water. I feel bold enough to ask a question under its protection. 'Mama, is my Papa dead like Olu's father?'

'Who told you that? Your father is in Sokoto with your brothers and sisters.'

I sit up quickly on my mat. I am curious about me. 'My brothers and sisters? Me?' My voice wavers. So I do have brothers and sisters. 'Then why don't I see them? Why don't I see my Papa and brothers and sisters? Malechi and *Elofunna* and the others live with their Mama and Papa, why do I just live with my Mama alone?'

Aunt Nnebogo yawns, and I hear the bed creak. She settles herself comfortably for the night.

'Do you want to go to Sokoto?'

'Yes!' I reply eagerly, with the ingratitude of an eleven-year-old.

'You will soon see your family, when you go to Ibusa for your mother's burial. Her *chi* must be laid to rest before your sister gets married.' Aunt Nnebogo's bed stops creaking, and I know she will answer no more questions. Children are not encouraged to talk directly to adults. That she has allowed this little dialogue to take place at all is just because we are alone in our room. She would have told me about the trip to Ibusa sooner or later, but it is the first time I am hearing of it and I am still not satisfied. Who is my mother? This question torments me.

Sleep has left me. All my senses are alive as if it were the beginning of a new day. But it is still dark. I make an elaborate bed for my Taiwo. I heap together on one side all my covering cloths, patting them loudly. I then make a hollow in the middle and put her in it. That is the only comfortable part of the mat, but I want my Taiwo to have it, so she can lie in comfort and listen to all my mutterings and questions. I move about noisily as I make all these preparations in the dark. I guess Aunt Nnebogo is not asleep, but is lying awake thinking. I know I have hurt her, but I so badly want to see my brothers and sisters in Sokoto. 'Wait until we tell Malechi tomorrow,' I whisper to my Taiwo. 'Ha, ha, you who have no father, uglying up our father. We have a father. He lives in Sokoto.' I go on clucking to my wooden Taiwo until quite late into the night.

I awake with a sensation of floating. It is bright daylight, and I feel as if the light is going to blind me. It forms a tunnel of oranges, blues and pinks, and I float through. As I go, the voice of a solo singer drifts towards me, accompanied by the gentle twanging of a *kora*. As I emerge, I see a group of women, wearing white shift-like garments, smiling and waving palm fronds as if in greeting. I hurry towards them, smiling and waving. Then I see my father. He is as I remember him, his arms open in welcome, urging me to come to him. Suddenly, I hear a low, piercing cry. A woman whose face I cannot see comes towards me. She holds her palm frond across my path to stop me. She has with her a little girl whom I immediately recognise. My Taiwo. 'No,' she says, 'go back. I have this one.' The woman indicates the little girl, who does not smile. 'Your father was coming to you, but you sent him back. He was coming to look after you because he feels guilty about not looking after you the last time. But you have refused to receive him. He wants you with him, but you have to go back. You have to learn to live without him.'

I try to push past her to go to my father. I suddenly realise how terribly I have missed him. I tell myself he did not deserve to die in the way he did. I must make it up to him. On my left the palm fronds still wave me on. The music intoxicates me, making me giddy.

'Help me send her back.' The voice of the faceless woman becomes a wail. Then the little girl smiles and waves, mouthing a farewell. Slowly, one after the other, the women join her, until my way is blocked, shutting me off from my father. I hear my father's voice, louder than the rest, wailing. I never like to hear men cry, least of all my father, whom I remember. I cannot remember my mother. But the woman turns and I see her face, a familiar face, like that of my sister Ifeyinwa. She holds out her palm-frond like a spear. 'Your mother refuses to let you die! Go back, my daughter. Your time is not yet.'

'Wake up, wake up, Kehinde!'

Kehinde's eyes fluttered open and focused on Albert's anxious face. Next to him was Moriammo, her face expressing concern. She leaned forward and said soothingly, 'Alby said he was coming to collect you, so as your friend, I say I go come. Now I am here. What do I find, enh? You shouting for your papa. Wake up, my sister, make we go home!'

31

Kehinde, her spirit still returning reluctantly from the other world, muttered, 'I just see my mama and papa.'

'Your parents wey done die since the year nineteen kererem? Wake up, now, I beg!'

'You lost a lot of blood,' Albert said quietly, with a tinge of guilt. Both the women looked at him, so he was momentarily confused. 'Can you manage?' he asked, to divert attention. It was obvious he was regretting the operation.

'Of course she can manage. Just wait outside, *oga*.' Moriammo took charge, helping Kehinde to dress. She was a little shaky. She glanced at the other bed, but it was empty. Leah had gone.

Kehinde spoke haltingly to Moriammo. 'The child I just flushed away was my father's *chi*, visiting me again. But I refused to allow him to stay in my body. It was a man-child.'

Moriammo looked at Kehinde, who could see she was worried. She was trying very hard to think of the right thing to say. Her brow furrowed and she smacked her lips. She bent towards Kehinde and said, 'Don't worry, my sister. Your father will come again. If not to you, he fit come to Bimpe as your grandchild. Just think of that.'

In the car, they drove in silence until they reached Moriammo's house. As she got down, she said, 'Take care, my sister. Rest well-o.'

As Albert started the car, Kehinde turned impulsively towards him.

'Albert, did they tell you the sex of the baby?'

'Hmmmmm, it was not a baby. It was an embryo that might have been a man-child.'

'And a man one day,' Kehinde added. Tactfully, Albert was silent. The silence was so long and brittle that Kehinde knew Albert was grieving. She wanted to find out more. 'If you have known it was a boy, Albert, would you have made me abort it?'

'You just want a quarrel and I'm not in the mood for it. What's done is done.'

'You didn't answer me Albert. You thought the child was a girl, didn't you? But I knew it would have been a boy. My father's *chi* was coming back to be with us. He was coming as my

32

child to look after me. I even saw my Taiwo and my mother.'
Albert looked at her sharply, but instead of speaking, he turned
on the music. He had never before refused to comfort Kehinde
when she needed it. She felt like a boat adrift on a stormy night,
lashed by the winds. Albert could not help her. How could he?
She was alone, in spite of what they said about marriage being
two people in one. It could not mean the same to him that the
child she had just flushed away was her father coming back.
Albert's imagination could not carry him that far. She glanced at
Albert as if he were a new person, his profile clear against the
window of the car. He had nothing to offer her.

Does Kehinde still love
albert?

7   *The Party*

'Send-off party?' Prahbu asked, tilting his head to one side, a habit that gave his listener the impression of indifference. But the look was deceptive. For behind his gold-rimmed glasses, his brown eyes twinkled with merriment and mischief. He loved going out to visit friends on the only half-day off he allowed his wife and himself. Though he and his wife Leila were Muslims, originally from Pakistan, they were very liberal. London Muslims, who would not say no to a drop of alcohol.

Prahbu knew perfectly well why Albert was giving the party and wished with all his might that he could stop him. 'You can still change your mind. You can still tell them you want your job back,' he said, hopefully.

Albert's profile against the window was a chiselled black human image against a greying light. But his smile was slow and wan. 'You mean I should return my superannuation and withdraw my resignation, Prahbu?' Albert was not completely devoid of humour. 'Our cultures in Nigeria put a lot of emphasis on home. The Yorubas say, "*Ori oye ki sun ta*" – the heir's head does not sleep outside, meaning the heir must always be buried in his father's compound.'

Prahbu rolled his head from side to side and intoned, 'I know, I know. But that was a long time ago. Suppose the heir went to war and died there, enh? All those things were very nice, nostalgic and romantic. But the truth is that they are no longer pragmatic. You must think pragmatically.' Prahbu exposed the palms of his hands as if the answer to everything unpragmatic lay inside them.

34

'But I want to go back to the way of life my father had, a life of comparative ease for men, where men were men and women were women, and one was respected as somebody. Here, I am nobody, just a storekeeper. I'm fed up with just listening to my wife and indulging her. The only alternative is to go to the pub, but going to stand among all those drunken whites is no solution. No, to be at home is better. There I can have my drink on the verandah, and people will pay attention to me, including my wife.'

Into Albert's memory came the image of his large, slow moving father as he was when Albert was growing up in Lagos. On Sundays, his father and his mates would put on crisp *agbadas* which their wives had spent the greater part of the week bleaching and starching. They would go from house to house visiting friends, drinking palm wine, eating kolanuts and dried fish. In this way they kept in touch with friends and relatives, caught up with home news and indulged in a little relaxation.

'But people always say that I am westernised,' Albert smiled wryly to himself. In fact, he played to perfection the role of the Igbo family man in London. But he was far from satisfied with its restrictions. Kehinde did not understand, but his sisters did. Kehinde would learn when they got home how she was supposed to behave. Here, she was full of herself, playing the role of a white, middle-class woman, forgetting she was not only black, but an Igbo woman, just because she worked in a bank and earned more than he did. Many women worked in banks at home, but did not allow it to go to their heads. Albert loved Kehinde, in his own way, but he needed room to breathe. As Kehinde was perfectly well aware, behind the veneer of westernisation, the traditional Igbo man was alive and strong, awaiting an opportunity to reclaim his birthright.

Prahbu, however, though well acquainted with the privileges of the traditional male, remained sceptical about their relevance to men like himself and Albert. He objected, 'I know what you mean, but that type of life is not possible here, in a country where a woman is Queen and where it's beginning to look as if we're soon going to have a woman Prime Minister. The trouble starts

35

when women get educated, and now it's too late to change back again.'

'Yes, but I want something more,' insisted Albert.

'Ah, ambition, ambition,' Prahbu said knowingly, opening his arms in a universal embrace. 'Well, you have the means now, with your superannuation and the money you'll get from the sale of your house.'

'I'm not selling the house right away. The superannuation – well, they've been very generous. I'm using part of it to ship the car and a few things in a container, but that will be after the send-off party. I'll leave two weeks after the party.'

'Isn't your wife going with you?'

'Oh no,' laughed Albert. 'That would be disastrous. We have to go back in the order in which we came to London.'

Prahbu could not hide his curiosity. Albert was willing to rehearse the plan for the removal of himself and his family from London.

'Lagos is like London, you know. It's difficult to get accommodation. When that's settled, I have to get a job, then look for a school for the children. My wife will stay on to sell the house.'

'Ah,' laughed Prahbu, 'but your wife came to London before your children were born, so she should go home before them.'

'You know your trouble, Prahbu, you are too meticulous. You and Leila will come to the party won't you?'

'Of course we'll come. Is it going to be one of those Nigerian parties where the host and hostess change their attire every hour and then all those invited are given presents?'

Albert allowed himself to laugh, almost with abandon. 'That's certainly how we do it in Lagos.'

'Must cost a lot of money.'

'Money is meant to be spent, Prahbu. And it's not every day you return to your homeland after almost eighteen years in London.'

Apart from Prahbu, Albert invited his white colleagues, his boss and the tea lady. They all accepted gladly and promised to come. He noticed that the white people felt honoured to be invited, whereas in Nigeria people feel that when they come to

36

you, they are honouring you. So the host feels gratified when his invitations are accepted. This was so in Albert's case, especially as he had cultivated the habit of saying very little at work.

He actually envied Kehinde and Moriammo the spontaneity of their relationship. They were never afraid of making mistakes and they seemed to forgive each other very quickly. Where would he find a man he could talk to like that?

Many of their friends and acquaintances came to the party. Kehinde, Moriammo and Amaka, the tenant's girlfriend, all worked very hard. Amaka, who had only recently arrived from Nigeria to join her boyfriend, Oseloke, was a jewel. She seemed to be everywhere at once, opening the door for guests, fetching drinks, or calming a little child. She would make a good wife for Oseloke.

Albert ran around mixing drinks, seeing to the music and accepting congratulations from friends. Many of his colleagues did not understand why he had decided to leave a secure job and go back, after putting in almost fifteen years' service in the same employment. But most of his country people living in Britain understood, and some even viewed him with envy. The picture of the life he would lead at home was very vivid in their imagination: taking his ease in a large, airy white bungalow, with white verandahs shaded by palm-fronds along drive, with easy laughter and more friends than you could count. The country was virtually swimming in oil, and oil meant money. Lucky Okolos.

Kehinde did not disappoint her friends. In the course of the evening, she changed clothes ten times, as rich men's wives did in Nigeria, to advertise their wealth and boost the ego of the man of the house. Albert, who, like Kehinde, had grown up in Lagos, loved to look expensive. He had been lavish with his superannuation money, so excited that the words simply tumbled out of his mouth: 'Make it the party of the year, K-k. I'm sure I'll get a job as soon as I get home. We may not even need to work again with the money from the sale of the house. The standard of living is not as high as it is here, but I shall work anyway.'

'It seems like yesterday that we arrived here,' Kehinde had

replied cautiously. 'We had nothing but youth and enthusiasm, and now look at us. Our shiny Jag parked outside our own house, our children . . . oh, sometimes I'm afraid that we're rushing things and may not be able to make it as fast in Nigeria as we have done here.'

'Of course we'll make it in Nigeria. It's our country, isn't it? One of the reasons I'm going ahead of you is to get us good accommodation, as befits our new image. If we all go together, it would mean squatting with relatives, and I can't imagine you liking that.'

Kehinde shook her head. She would not like that.

'Then look your best. And don't forget to buy little presents for our guests, just as we do at home. As I said, I want people to remember the party Albert Okolo gave when he was leaving London.'

Kehinde did not let Albert down. She treated her guests to the whole array of Nigerian traditional styles and fabrics, from guinea *boubou* to *aso-oke iro* and *buba*, to the Igbo lace blouse and George *lappa*, ending with the Igbo ceremonial costume of white *otu-ogwu*. This consisted of a cloth wound around her body beneath the armpits, leaving her shoulders bare. Precious coral beads adorned her neck, hair and ears. The outfit was to emphasise her position as first wife of the first son, and the mother of a son herself. Kehinde revelled in the impression she created.

Among the guests was Mary Elikwu, who, with her husband, was a former friend of Albert and Kehinde. Mary had recently left her husband because, she claimed, he beat her. She had taken her six children with her. To the men in their circle, she was a curiosity, to the women, a kind of challenge. To Kehinde she was a fallen woman who had no sense of decorum. Kehinde was going to 'forget' to invite her, but Albert had announced the party at their local Igbo family meeting. When Mary Elikwu approached Kehinde at the party, Kehinde became rigid. Mary, who was a university graduate and was known to disapprove of overdressing, started to finger the coral beads. She commented, 'One would have thought you were just getting married.'

'What would you have done if your husband had provided them for you? Wouldn't you have worn them?' Kehinde opened her big eyes and looked her pointedly up and down. Kehinde thought Mary Elikwu looked ridiculous in her plain white Marks and Spencers blouse and a no-longer fashionable George *lappa*. The cheek of it. She wondered again why Albert had invited her – a woman who refused to work at her marriage.

Mary Elikwu was surprised at Kehinde's reaction. She had meant to pay her a compliment, but she was learning very fast that a woman who left her marriage would always be marginalised, even by those she and her husband had regarded as close friends. She heard her own voice saying, 'I'm sorry Kehinde. I meant well, believe me. They are lovely clothes.'

'Mrs Okolo, if you please,' Kehinde snapped, elongating her rather short, thick neck as far as it would go to show her coral beads to advantage.

'Oh, but you can call me Mary,' Mary Elikwu persisted, instead of going away to hide her face in a corner as Kehinde would have preferred. 'Professionally, I don't even use my husband's name. I prefer to use Jackson.' Mary appeared unaware that her attempts to mollify Kehinde were only infuriating her more. Her last remark had succeeded in alienating her completely.

'What is the matter with this woman?' Kehinde wondered. 'Not wanting to be called "Mrs", when every Nigerian woman is dying for the title. Even professors or doctors or heads of companies still call themselves "Professor (Mrs)" or "Dr (Mrs)". This woman must be crazy. Is she bigger than all of them then? I don't understand her.'

'Mrs Okolo, Mrs Okolo,' called Amaka from the kitchen. 'Please ma, come and tell me how you want this *moyin-moyin* served.'

Kehinde swept past Mary Elikwu into the kitchen, sucking her teeth as she went. The woman must be jealous, she told herself, feeling gratified at her own explanation. For all her qualifications, she, Kehinde, was worth more than a woman like Mary Elikwu who couldn't even keep her husband.

Kehinde was still in her *oto-ogwu* as she stood by the door, Albert holding her hand, just like a western couple. On a nearby chair was a huge basket, containing beautiful wrapped gifts for the guests. Kehinde dipped her free hand into the basket and gave each person a parcel as they left. Some had pyrex plates, others a long-playing record, or a bottle of expensive wine. Everybody took something home, as if it were a real Nigerian party.

The last to leave were Moriammo and her husband, Tunde, still wearing their social faces as they said good-bye. Like many Africans in London, over the years they had learned to tell people exactly what they wanted to hear, and it had become second nature. As they closed the front door, Kehinde bent down to remove her shoes. They were expensive hand-sewn suede, but they hurt. She was not a slim woman, and she had been standing all evening. However, Kehinde did not mind the pain, since the desired effect had been achieved.

Albert was delighted with himself, his family and the party. He extended his arms and invited airily, 'Come into my arms Mrs Kehinde Okolo.' He caught Kehinde and began to dance with her, singing Bonnie Mack's hit, 'My sweetie, my sugar'. This was so unexpected that Kehinde dropped the shoes she had just taken off. 'Are you all right, Alby? Make you control yourself-o. The pikin dey upstairs, or you don forget am? Me sef, I for start to pack the glasses, before I go sleep.'

'Make you leave all that, boh. Come now, madam wife.'

Albert propelled her into their downstairs bedroom. Kehinde was too weary to offer any resistance, worn out from wearing a social mask, talking nonsense and being a hostess. She noticed the lightness of Albert's touch, his playfulness, and his impatience. He did not pretend to satisfy her first. He was very sure of himself, like a little boy released from school. Before she could begin to take pleasure in it, he had finished and fallen asleep.

Though her body was exhausted, Kehinde found herself too keyed up to sleep. She lay in the dark and thought about the change that was coming over Albert, remembering their early days together. Unlike many Nigerian men, he had adapted easily to the cultural dictates of England. He had come to London in 1960, and sent for Kehinde a year later, when she was eighteen and working in a bank in Lagos. When she came to England, she got a job in a bank again. Through in-service training, she rose from desk cashier to assistant manager in a little over ten years. Albert rose in his job too.

During those years they also had Joshua and Bimpe. Kehinde had seen the way her sister Ifeyinwa lived, and she knew how her mother had died, so was not anxious for a big family. She was quite content, and even the news of her father's death did not affect her for long. Similarly, news of increased violence and repeated coups in Nigeria had little impact. They assumed they would return eventually and build their own house in Ibusa, their home village.

Kehinde could not pinpoint exactly when Albert's sisters had begun to exert an influence over their marriage. Their letters and the newspapers seemed to be full of Nigeria's oil boom, but as far as Kehinde was concerned, they were doing fine in London and had no reason to go back. They loved parties and went out frequently in the old Jaguar, which Albert washed and polished every Friday evening. Sitting in the passenger seat beside Albert, with the car stereo playing Sunny Ade or Bob Marley, Kehinde did not worry much about what else was happening in the world.

Kehinde's thoughts came abruptly back to the present. She was conscious of unease about Albert's new-found confidence, and found herself reluctantly wondering how Mary Elikwu coped on her own. She had worked so hard for the party, soon after agreeing to undergo the abortion and to put the house up for sale, that she felt she deserved more consideration than Albert was giving her. She had hoped all the concessions she had made would bring them closer than before, but instead she felt Albert slipping through her fingers, like melting ice. It looked as if she was the only one in the family satisfied with their stay in England. Albert could hardly hide his delight at the thought of going home, and the children had been infected with his enthusiasm. Kehinde wondered why she found it so difficult to join in.

41

And why did he make love to her like that, as if she had no desires to be satisfied? Especially as he would be leaving in a matter of weeks. Fifteen years was a long time to invest in a project and still not be sure of it. Kehinde told herself she was being foolish to feel so insecure all of a sudden. She turned over to sleep, resolving to take each day as it came.

8 Albert's Letters

The phone rang. Kehinde picked it up and listened for a moment before erupting irritably: 'All right, so you're coming tomorrow? I'm fed up with all these people nosing around. Yes, of course I want to sell the house, but I'm sure that couple last week were just having a day out. You should tell people that this is not a furniture shop . . . Yes, I know, but that doesn't mean that every Tom, Dick and Harry has the right to invade my privacy . . . All right, I'll show them around.' Kehinde let the receiver fall noisily, accompanied by the sucking of her teeth.

'You should have let Dad sell the house before he left,' said Joshua, adding to her annoyance.

'Mum can sell it too if she wants,' Bimpe defended her.

'Can she? People have been coming and going for months and not buying. I bet Dad would have sold it just like that,' Joshua said, clicking his fingers.

'Mum can do it too.' Bimpe's voice took on a dangerously low tone. Kehinde knew that if she allowed the argument to continue, Bimpe would soon burst into tears. The children missed their father and so did she.

'Stop it you two! Help get the tea, Joshua. Boil the rice so we can have it with the fish stew in the fridge.'

'Just because Dad has left, you don't care who cooks the tea any more.'

'Don't worry me this evening, you hear me Joshua? I thought you liked rice. So why can't you boil enough for all of us? It will take the same time. What are you grumbling about? I'll come and warm the stew for you if that will make you feel better.'

43

'In some London families, boys don't cook rice.' Joshua slouched out of the kitchen, muttering to himself.

'Aunty, aunty, I'm back. How was your day?' Amaka's voice vibrated from the hallway.

'That woman's twangy voice . . . shio,' Joshua complained loudly, not caring whether Amaka heard him or not.

Bimpe hurriedly shut him out of the kitchen and looked at her mother. They laughed in sympathy with each other.

Kehinde went into the hallway to talk to Amaka, who had good news. She had been accepted in a nursing school. She was very excited. She had come to England to be with her childhood sweetheart, and soon after, they had agreed to get married. He would finish his advertising course and both of them would then go home. Nigeria had even awarded him a scholarship to hasten his success. The Oselokes' future was bright.

Before Albert left, he had asked Oseloke, Amaka's husband, to help with the upkeep of the house. It was understood the Oselokes would move out as soon as Kehinde found a buyer. Six months later, the roof had developed a leak, which Kehinde could not afford to have fixed. She had hoped Albert would send money from Nigeria. According to the people she heard from, money was flowing in Nigeria like water, as a result of the oil boom. Kehinde believed it when she thought of the extravagance of Festac '77, the pan-African festival of arts and culture, held in Lagos.

For once, Kehinde was ready to admit to envy. She knew it would be disastrous to let people know how she felt, but all her confidence was slipping away. A few months before, Amaka would not have dared shout for her from the hallway. Now, not only did she shout, but Kehinde was happy to be called to hear her good news.

To think that she and Albert had pitied them when they first came, protecting them from the immigration officers. Oseloke had been an illegal immigrant, but by the time the authorities caught up with him, he had become a student on scholarship, with a part-time job and a social security number. When Amaka

44

came to join him, she came to join a boyfriend who was already settled in London, and marriage made it possible for her to stay.

Like Albert, they did not want to stay longer than necessary. They never stopped talking about Nigeria, the friendliness, the money, the carefree attitude. Albert had been carried away on a tide of optimism which had now reached the children too. They talked constantly of seeing their Daddy and Aunt Selina.

Kehinde swallowed her feelings and listened to Amaka's good-luck story, making the expected congratulatory noises. At least they would soon leave for Nigeria, she told herself.

Shortly after, a letter came from Albert. Like most of his letters, it read like the lists of dispatches he used to make at his former workplace in the East London docks. She was to get the children ready; she was to make sure they had had all their injections; she should get them a dozen pairs of socks and a dozen pairs of knickers. The enclosed tickets were for them. He had got them places in a nice private school, where they could study in peace with few distractions.

Kehinde knew that this meant a boarding school, the automatic choice of the elite in Nigeria. Looking back at her life at Mount Carmel Convent School, Kehinde decided that a few years in a place like that would do Bimpe and Joshua good. But she was going to miss them.

When she told the children, they were delighted. If she had nourished a faint hope that they would protest, she was disappointed. Apart from their stay with a foster parent when they were little, they had never travelled anywhere, and had listened with curiosity to their friends' accounts of holiday experiences. Now they were promised a real adventure. In spite of herself, Kehinde felt their reaction as a betrayal. Did they have no feeling for her at all? She had to convince herself it would be good for them to experience Nigerian life.

A few days after they left, Kehinde started to become aware again of that intrusive inner voice, the voice of her dead twin, Taiwo. She was very much alone, with no one to confide her anxieties in. Moriammo, with whom she could have talked things over, had just given birth to a baby boy, and was immersed in

45

motherhood and Tunde's devoted attention. Kehinde could not even visit her without his hovering presence. The birth of the baby had altered Tunde, and Moriammo was basking in their newly affectionate relationship. It heightened Kehinde's sense of her own isolation, her feeling of being marginal to everyone else's lives. Because of this, Taiwo's voice was strong within her, articulating her vaguely-acknowledged fears. 'Why do Albert's letters say nothing? What is he hiding? Why does Ifeyinwa suddenly never write any more?' It was a year now since he had left. The dream she had had at the hospital came back to her, and Taiwo's voice: 'See, our father was coming to protect you from this, but you killed him. Do you think your Alby can live alone all this time? Who do you imagine is giving him the attention he needs to survive?' Kehinde sometimes felt she was on the verge of madness. To dispel the voice, she would burst into a hymn, 'Sweet sacrament of peace', singing it loudly, over and over again. But when she stopped, the voice would be there. 'Why don't you go to Nigeria and find out what is happening, before it's too late? Have you forgotten that in Nigeria it's considered manly for men to be unfaithful? Even if he didn't want women they would come to him.'

'But I have to sell the house first. And why do I have to justify myself to you? Why don't you go away and stay dead!'

'Aunty, aunty are you all right?' came Amaka's solicitous voice.

Kehinde laughed apologetically. 'Don't mind me. I think I'm beginning to miss my family. Now I talk to myself about the sale of the house.'

'Ah, aunty. Your family is not just the children and Mr Okolo. What of us, aren't we your family too? You can talk to me, to us if you like. It's not good to talk to yourself.' Amaka looked like the nurse she had become.

'It's not quite like that. But never mind, you wouldn't understand.'

Kehinde began secretly to make plans to go. She knew that to leave a house of that size half empty would be wasteful and foolish. She settled Amaka and her husband in the largest room

46

upstairs and advertised for a tenant for the two smaller rooms. She accepted the first response that came.

The new tenant, Michael Gibson, worked at the local community centre. He was well-spoken and polite, and though he was black, was from the Caribbean. She liked his gentleness but told herself that he would not stay long. A single black man in a good job was too precious a commodity to be overlooked. There must be a catch somewhere, but as long as he paid his rent on time, Kehinde was not going to be curious. Somewhere at the back of her mind she had prayed for a female tenant, and had hesitated at first, especially as the man was not a Nigerian. Within a few days of his moving in, she did not understand why she had harboured this fear in the first place. Was it because people – her people – would say: 'Look, she's taken a new tenant into her house and the tenant is a man and a foreigner'? She and Albert had never had much to do with their fellow black people who were not Nigerians. Anyway, she reasoned, as Oseloke and Amaka were there too, the arrangement was decent enough. No one would be able to accuse her of working and living for herself alone. She was going to buy more western luxuries she knew she would need to establish herself as the been-to madam of the house – essentials like a washing machine, a fridge, a television and a video recorder. As for a music centre, she would buy the biggest and loudest she could afford.

But suppose, just suppose after all this, Albert had acquired a girlfriend or been unfaithful? Her mischievous *chi*, in the voice of Taiwo, had been hinting as much. How would she take it?

Albert was not like that, she told herself. She knew him through and through. He was different, he had principles, and the major one of these was to keep his family happy. No, Albert was not the type to break apart his family, or to make her unhappy. The voice of Taiwo was simply being mischievous.

Moreover, Nigeria was her country too. She could not have changed that much! Which Nigerian girlfriend would be able to stand the presence of a rich, been-to madam? They wouldn't dare compete with her! And as for Albert's letters, he had never been much of a letter writer, even when he was courting her.

47

First she had to sell the house, but that too was proving slow and stressful. The 'For Sale' sign at the front of the house flapped about in the wind reminding her of her failure.

The sound of the front door being gently closed woke her from her daydreaming. It was Michael Gibson. He had a habit of saying by way of greeting, 'It's only me,' as he walked into the kitchen.

'Good evening, Mrs Okolo.'

'Good evening, Mr Gibson. Had a nice day?'

'Mustn't grumble.'

To judge by his expressions, Michael Gibson had been in Britain a long time. Like the Okolos, he was a fairly well educated black person in a lower middle-class job. Kehinde sometimes wondered what his story was, why an attractive black man of over thirty was living alone, and a black man with a good job besides. Many black men could not stand routine for long, and they reacted more violently to the inevitable racism than women. This man, on the contrary, was calm and considerate, as he would need to be to keep his job as a community worker.

Like the Oselokes, Michael Gibson promised to move as soon as Kehinde got a buyer, and she accordingly reduced the rent. He was allowed to use the kitchen, but he never did. He made his tea and coffee in his room and ate out, even on Sundays. Black men know how to waste money, Kehinde thought.

'You know, Mrs Okolo, the weather was kind today.'

Kehinde had not realised he was still standing there in the hallway, wading through the free advertising papers shoved through the doors of most London homes. He must have been watching her. She infused some life into her voice and answered cheerfully. 'Yes, the sun really shone today. I felt hot, for once.'

Michael Gibson laughed politely. 'You had a good day then?'

'Yes, Mr Gibson, thank you.'

This short conversation snapped her out of her gloom. Michael Gibson made his way thoughtfully upstairs and Kehinde went into the front room to see if she could have a chat with Moriammo over the telephone. The kitchen would then be vacant for Mr Gibson, just in case he wanted to use it, but he did not.

With Moriammo, Kehinde was luckier. Tunde was not at home, so they talked for two hours, and she felt lighter. The telephone bill was her business, after all.

Weeks later, letters came from Joshua and Bimpe. They were in a private school, and were enjoying themselves. In Joshua's school, they were building their own toilets, and each class had a piece of land for farming, so the school did not have to buy eggs and vegetables. Their father had been to see them the previous Saturday. Bimpe observed: 'There are so many aunties here, some even live in our house. I like it, but you must come soon. Even if you can't sell the house, just come and see Dad and your relations. Your sister Aunty Ifi is lovely.'

A few days later, a letter from Albert followed. 'The streets of Lagos are like Petticoat Lane on a Sunday,' he said. 'Social life is great. My new job entails my travelling to the north, places like Kano, Maiduguri and Kaduna. I cannot send money from here because, after all K, you are in a good job, and should be able to pay the bills from your income. Are the Oselokes no longer there? K, you just have to learn to manage better. Take care, Alby.'

9 Moriammo's Visit

'It's only me.'

'Who be dat, K?' Moriammo asked.

'My new tenant,' Kehinde replied, kicking her friend's foot.

'Ouch! I no know say you done get a new one. This one na *man*, K!'

'I no tell you the other night for telephone? You no dey listen. Shush now, I beg, he dey for house! . . . Mr Gibson, this is my friend Moriammo. We used to work together in the bank in Crouch End.'

Michael Gibson removed his hat and said with a slight bow, 'Good evening madam.' At the same time he turned to Kehinde and asked, 'How are you today, Mrs Okolo?'

'I'm fine. Had a nice day?'

'Mustn't grumble.'

Moriammo's face was a picture. She was studying Gibson's well laundered clothes, close cropped hair and very clean hands. She arched her brows, signifying: 'I'd be worried about what people will say if I were you.'

'You're not me,' Kehinde said. 'The Oselokes dey here, or you don forget?'

'I no say nothing, my sister. Only his hands too clean for a man. You know say we don dey used to rough hard-working African men's hands. With hands so smooth he go fit do the ting properly?'

'Honestly, Moriammo, you are a shame to good Muslim womanhood!'

They both laughed.

'They can't win can they? When they are dirty, we say they are dirty. When they are clean we complain in case they outdo us. Maybe that's why some of them are now turning white and not getting married,' Kehinde observed.

'You mean dis nice man here no get wife yet? Oh, ho, ho, what you have here-o, Kehinde? I no trust men wey perfume dem body, you know.'

'What are you talking about, Moriammo? Allah dey! I never tink of dat. I see, I see. No wonder.'

'Oh no, I no dey suggest anyting. I was just about to say . . .'

'Make you no say,' Kehinde emphasised seriously, opening the palms of her hands in front of Moriammo's face to keep her quiet. Instead, Kehinde served the friend plantain and chicken. Being alone, they ate without attention to decorum, smacking their lips like children eating stolen food. There was no one there to tell them not to eat in the front room.

'I don't like the tone of Alby's letters. He seems to be settling . . . you know, very well without me. He writes, but does not say much.'

Sebi 'I warned you' ruins friendship, Moriammo thought. Instead of talking, she filled her mouth with juicy plantain. She studied Kehinde's face to see how she would take it, as Kehinde was no longer someone she would tell only what she wanted to hear. Their friendship had been through too much for that. 'Then why you no go Lagos, go join Alby? I tell you say, the girls there dey craze for any man wey just return from England!'

'But Nigeria na country where dem dey paper-qualification mad. All this in-service training and experience wey I dey get here no go mean nothing, you know,' Kehinde explained despairingly.

'Eno be dat bad, I tell you. You fit get job in another Barclays bank. E go just be like a transfer to you – from one Barclays bank to another.'

'Where you de all the time, Moriammo? We no get Barclays any more. Na Union bank now. Nigeria don boycott Barclays because of that trouble for South Africa.'

'Haba! All this trouble sef!' Moriammo chewed thoughtfully.

51

'But I sure say you go get another job. And if not, stay home and play the big Madam and chop life. Plenty oyinbo women dey do am all the time. Alby get good job. And you go don save your marriage. Na dat one important most you know. Woman wey no get husband na embarrassment for everybody. Well, sebi you know dat already?'

Kehinde did not want to be an embarrassment to anybody. When she went home, it would be to save her marriage. Yet, though the voice of her Taiwo was urging her to go, her rational self was saying that there was no need to panic. She knew her Alby. One year in Nigeria could not have changed him that much.

Kehinde imagined how it would feel to be completely dependent on Albert, a situation that would be quite strange to her. How could she expect Albert to take care of all her financial needs, just because she was married to him? And with all his sisters and relations watching? It was too un-African. For an Igbo woman, her capacity for work is her greatest asset. If she was not seen to be productive, she could imagine a situation in which Albert might be persuaded to discard her, but he would never give in to such pressure.

'What situation you dey mumble about? *Abi*, you don begin talk to your second now in old age? Dem say twins sabi talk to demselves plenty, plenty time.'

Kehinde laughed lightly to cover her embarrassment. 'No, I just dey say we never depend on our husbands financially. At least my Mama never did.'

'How you know? Your Mama die when you be small pikin. Go home, go relax. Be a been-to Madam. Put your feet up. Be a white woman. Make you enjoy the sunshine. There go be plenty of servants too. So what's your trouble, enh?'

'So wetin you tink say I be? I no be Igbo woman?'

'I know who you be. Igbo woman who no go happy until she dey work and work and carry the burden of the whole world. All that work, work dey give us power?'

Kehinde regarded her friend with respect. Moriammo had more depth than she realised. It was Moriammo who was now embarrassed. The two women, though such close friends, hid their underbellies. They laughed, high ringing laughter that lacked conviction. Moriammo quickly took refuge in empty banter: 'The world is turning upside down. I feel am in my bones.'

'No, na full circle the world de turn. After all, they say e dey go round and round. Now most oyinbo women I know done dey work, like we do.'

'Na true-o. You know K, I no like chicken wey no get pepper. Not enough pepper for this your chicken. Chicken without pepper give you heartburn.' Moriammo was determined to go back to mundane things.

'Where you read that?'

'Where I read am? Na from Encyclopaedia Worldcanica.'

'Oh my God Moriammo. You are murdering the English language.'

'I didn't ask them to come to Lagos and force am down my throat. I beg bring some pepper. Make I no throw up.'

Kehinde went into the kitchen and came back with a jar of good Ghana pepper sauce, which she plonked on the floor where they were eating, their legs spread wide.

With Taiwo's mischievous spirit in her, Kehinde put on one of Albert's 'naughty' videos. They screamed with laughter and woke Olumide, Moriammo's baby, who was tucked away warmly in the corner of the couch. He had been so good that they had almost forgotten him, but he began to make a fuss as if to make up for lost time. Moriammo wiped the pepper off her hand with kitchen paper and picked him up.

'I'll go and warm his bottle. That baby makes so much palava, enh?'

'We go soon go home though. He don dey so good today. Just slept through all that nonsense we been dey watch. But those people dey craze, bah! Olumide na good boy. E no go tell him papa.'

'If Olumide tell am, e go get convulsion.'

'Na only convulsion him go get? The shock fit kill am.'

Mischief was dancing in Moriammo's eyes as she picked up her baby.

Outside, it was not dark, but it was nearing evening. The two women looked in every direction, before turning to stare at each other. Where was the baby's pram? It had been left just outside, in the porch.

'Yeh, K, wey the baby pram?' Moriammo found her tongue. Kehinde handed her the baby's blanket which she had been clutching to her chest as if for comfort. She ran down the street, stifling the urge to shout. She was in England, and in England you suffer in silence. No pram, only closed doors and parked cars, and a few skeletal trees. One or two people passed, not looking at them, but there was no pram.

Kehinde returned to where Moriammo was standing by the door, holding the baby. Voices were raised, Amaka's above the others. Oseloke and Michael Gibson had also emerged, and they were all talking angrily. The expensive blue pram had vanished into thin air.

'I can't believe this, I just can't.' Kehinde looked at Moriammo, who stared back at her, still clutching Olumide to her chest. Her eyes were red, and her lips were chalky from dryness. Neither of them underestimated the scale of the disaster, or what Tunde's reaction would be.

Moriammo had two girls, aged eleven and nine. When Kehinde told her that morning at the Wimpy that she was pregnant, she too had decided to try her luck. She had coerced Tunde, who was a lazy and reluctant lover. Moriammo had never seen or heard of a man like that. If he had been white, and could have looked after himself properly, he would not have bothered with marriage at all. But his mother would not hear of such an abomination. Somebody had you so you must give birth to somebody else, the world goes round that way.

Moriammo persisted. She forced herself on him. She threatened not to cook for him. But she only succeeded when she threatened to write to her people telling them that her husband was impotent. Potency is an essential attribute of the Nigerian man, and Tunde would do anything to establish his virility and

54

avoid the humiliation of his wife going about saying 'he no fit do nothing for bed.' That she wanted another child, he knew, but what if the child was another girl. What would he do? How could a man live sanely in a house full of women? But it was better to give in and risk having a girl-child than face Moriammo's taunts. He gave her what she wanted in an absent-minded way. Moriammo paid him no mind as long as she became pregnant. Her everyday life was so full of other activities, that it hardly bothered her that their marriage was only a convenience. Over the years she had become accustomed to sleeping soundly at night, and was even grateful that he did not make demands on her. In spite of Tunde's poor performance, she became pregnant almost at once. Then Kehinde and her husband decided they were going to abort their child. Before she was able to gather her thoughts and advise her friend to think again, they had already done it, and all she could do was comfort Kehinde, riddled with guilt. Being a Muslim, she was surprised at them, because Alby and Kehinde seemed so close, touching and joking openly, no matter who was watching. Moriammo had thought that because Albert was a Christian, he could be relied on to treat Kehinde with respect.

To say that Tunde was beside himself with joy the day baby Olumide was born would be an understatement. He was wild. He telephoned all their friends, both in England and Nigeria, and started calling himself 'Tunde and Sons Ltd'. Presents came from everywhere. The day the child was named, they invited as many people as if it were a wedding, and rented a suite at the London Park Hotel for the reception. The baby's picture was in all the Nigerian papers in London: Olumide – 'my saviour, my standard bearer, my warrior is here'. Nothing was too good for him. Moriammo was to take a whole year off to look after him, so he would not be exposed to the dangers of child minders.

Tunde never gave Moriammo money for housekeeping. He contributed ten pounds a week for meat, except the weeks when he would kill four or five of the rabbits they bred in their backyard. But for his son Olumide, he bought the most expensive pram in their local Mothercare shop. Moriammo quailed at what he would do and say when he heard it was gone.

'I think we'd better call the police,' Gibson suggested.

'Yes, do that, but I must go home now,' Moriammo said anxiously.

'What type of neighbourhood is this?' Amaka's voice rang out.

'They steal anything.' Kehinde's voice was apologetic.

'Why did you not put it inside the corridor? Those big prams cost a fortune these days,' Michael Gibson sympathised.

'I'm going to be on the look out for it,' Kehinde promised.

Moriammo, cradling her baby in her arms, went home in a mini cab, which Gibson had managed to call in spite of the chaos. It was a short distance, but Gibson insisted on Moriammo going by car. 'It's getting dark and you're upset,' he persuaded her.

Moriammo was so distressed that without thinking she told Tunde all that happened. She had known he would be angry, but if she could have anticipated the form his rage would take, she would have kept quiet and replaced the pram with her own money. But she was in shock, and she wanted to tell Tunde about it. Since Olumide's birth, they had achieved a kind of closeness which had not been in their marriage before. As a result, she had caught herself more than once confiding in Tunde things she would formerly have kept to herself. She knew this was taking a risk as Tunde, coming from a Muslim family, could conceivably take other wives, and what would happen to her secrets then? Besides, it would not have been easy to conceal the loss of the pram, as Tunde, seeing her getting out of the cab, rushed to open the door in consternation.

The result was that he banned her from visiting Kehinde, with a series of unanswerable questions. What were they doing that they forgot his child's pram? What was Moriammo, a good Muslim wife, doing at all, with a woman who had sent all her family away so she could have a good time? Any man could go to her now, had Moriammo thought of that? What would Olumide think of her when he grew up?

Moriammo was too confused and shocked to stand up for her

56

friend. Tunde's words were too coruscating for her to attempt to intervene, as he vomited his pent-up envy of the Okolos. He spoke with contempt of the inadequacies of men like Albert, who leave their wives at the mercy of all-comers in London, who take their wives to clinics to abort their babies because of money. Why did he go back to Nigeria when they both had good jobs? It was because of greed and the love of women. It was obvious Alby must have another woman by now, and had no further use for Kehinde. No doubt he was trying to leave his wife discreetly since he had never been able to stand up to her. All that hand-holding in public was for show. And meanwhile Moriammo, the mother of Tunde's heir and a respectable Muslim woman, had allowed her to be seen in such a compromising situation . . .

'Tunde, Tunde! Why don't you stop and take a breath,' Moriammo at last summoned enough self-respect to object. 'It's only a pram after all.'

'Did your father know what a pram is?' Tunde spat back.

Moriammo was silent. She was too hurt to pursue the argument, and Olumide needed her attention. Tunde, meanwhile, continued to pour a stream of vituperation on the worthless Okolos.

10   Departure

Everybody was surprised at Kehinde's sudden decision to go back to Lagos after her initial ambivalence. She now adopted the position that Albert could come back and sell the house himself. She was no longer going to stay in London, laying herself open to anyone who cared to ugly her name, simply because she was not under a man's protection.

Look at Moriammo, her friend! She had suddenly become too busy to answer the telephone. When Kehinde called at the house in person, it was Tunde who opened the door, informing her that Moriammo had gone to see an aunt – when Kehinde had never heard of an aunt before. Nevertheless, she started trying to explain the loss of the pram, but Tunde swept her aside with a condescending wave. Under his gaze she felt small and humiliated, but for her friend, Moriammo's, sake, she did not react. She did, however, feel the injustice. She had not asked the thief to come and tow the pram away, so why was she being punished?

She realised how far towards the hem of existence she had been pushed when she invited a handful of friends to celebrate her birthday. Several did not even bother to telephone their apologies, to say nothing of coming. Amaka, her husband, Michael Gibson and a few others she saw frequently were the only ones to honour her invitation. It prompted Michael Gibson to remark with concern, 'And the lady with the pram, she couldn't come to your party?'

'It was not a party,' snapped Kehinde, 'just a small get-together.' She was too hurt to do anything but hiss 'And I didn't invite her anyway.' Gibson withdrew, wondering what the differ-

58

ence was between a get-together and a party. He could not know that Kehinde's mind had gone back to the lavish farewell party they had thrown for Albert's departure: the food, the clothes, the music . . . It seemed to have happened centuries ago, but it was barely two years. She was amazed at how short people's memories were. She had been a generous hostess to their friends, but where were those friends now?

It seemed that without Albert, she was a half-person. Unable to cope with the nagging silence, she plunged into depression, which was accentuated when Amaka, of all people, took it upon herself to pity her. 'You look awful today, are you all right, Mummy?' In Nigeria, calling a slightly older woman Mummy was a term of endearment, showing that the person so addressed was as dear as one's own mother, but here in London, it rattled Kehinde. Why had Amaka just started calling her that? It was out of place in an environment where anything connected with getting old was taboo. She could not say, 'Amaka, please don't call me Mummy. I'm not old enough to be your mother.' She would sound pathetic and ridiculous. Kehinde even imagined what Amaka and her husband would say about her. 'I called Kehinde "Mummy" today, and she said, "I am not your mother."' Laughter, and Oseloke's response, 'Boh, she is getting old. She perhaps no realize dat.'

No, she would not let her insecurity show. She would hold her head up, like an Igbo woman, one with the spirits of two women in her.

A week later, she bumped into Moriammo. Perhaps it was her imagination, but Moriammo behaved like a child caught stealing a piece of meat from her mother's cooking pot. Kehinde chased her, calling after her: 'Olumide's mother, Moriammo! Why now? What have I done?' She caught up with her and held her hand, noticing that Moriammo looked a little dishevelled. Well, Kehinde could understand, she was still at home looking after Olumide. And Tunde did not approve of women dressing up just to go to the market to buy meat and okro. Kehinde recalled his joke: 'Okro and meat no mind the way you look!' Olumide must have brought them closer again, as boy babies were wont to do.

At last, Moriammo was becoming the good Muslim wife Tunde had always wanted her to be. Who was she to intrude into their harmony?

Kehinde felt again that she was sitting at the hem of life, looking in and not belonging, but for old time's sake, she was going to find out why. This was not Amaka, a woman too young to challenge. 'Moriammo, long time no see. You no even come my birthday party. Why now, friend?'

'But I sent card ke, *abi*, you no get am?'

'Card? Who wan' card. If I wan' card, I go buy for myself. Plenty, plenty cards de for inside shops. Na you I wan', not cards. Wetin I do you, friend?'

Tears, unbidden, streamed down Moriammo's face. They were in the middle of the pavement with shoppers scurrying around them. A butcher, in front of whose shop they were standing, came out in his blood-stained apron to ask, 'Can you move on please? You're blocking my shop window, see?'

Between the butcher's shop and the sub-post office kept by an Asian family there was a little alley way, and without a word they moved into it. Neither of them was in any mood to argue with the butcher, whose arms had already been akimbo, ready for a fight.

In the relative privacy of their alley, Moriammo's tongue was freed. She rattled out most of the unflattering things Tunde had said the night the pram was stolen, not having the presence of mind to censor anything.

Kehinde was dumbstruck. So, all those years, Tunde had only been tolerating Albert and herself. But why? They were no better off, or at the most only slightly. So why the bitterness? Kehinde had lost track of Moriammo's monologue when she heard her say, 'I'll give you a call soon. I must go.' She scurried off and disappeared into the market crowd.

'Thank God she didn't say she was sorry, that would have killed me. Moriammo,' Kehinde mourned aloud, 'how long have I known you? Almost twenty years, during which we hurt and forgave each other more than the proverbial forty-nine times nine.'

Another fifty years would not erase the shock she felt that damp Saturday morning in Stratford street market. The world was suddenly much more complicated than it had seemed hitherto. She was now a fallen woman, like the street walker she had condemned when she was covered in furs and purring like a spoilt cat in Albert's Jaguar. Wondering what that woman's story was, she had forgotten what she originally went out to buy. Her shoes felt heavy. Was it Albert's fault, or hers, that she found herself in this position? She had not committed a crime, so why was she being cast as the guilty party? She had not deserted her husband, he had just gone home ahead of her, to start building their new life in Nigeria. She was a part of that life, and would soon be reunited with Albert.

She stretched her hand out many times before she eventually had the courage to phone Mary Elikwu. She had no idea what she was going to talk to her about. Was she going to ask her what it meant to be rejected? She began to understand how widows feel, not only at the loss of their husbands but also their friends. As the phone rang, Kehinde began to feel unsure of herself, remembering the way she had treated Mary Elikwu at the party. She was about to replace the receiver when a child picked up the telephone, announcing breathlessly that Mummy had gone to demonstrate for free milk.

'Free milk? What free milk?'

There was a struggle over the line. An older child took the receiver and spoke politely: 'Sorry, Madam. Mother is a member of our local One Parent Family Group and the Prime Minister is cutting our free milk. All the parents are meeting to plan a campaign. Who shall I say called, Aunty?'

'Just say Kehinde Okolo called.' As she put down the receiver, she was conscious of relief that Mary had not been there.

The following Monday, Kehinde gave in her notice at work. Her few white women colleagues were aghast, as Kehinde was good at her job, and seemed happy, too. She had long learnt not to be too sensitive to their cynical innuendos. She had thought, when Moriammo went home to have her baby, that she would be lonely, but she had not been. She had simply started spending her lunch hour with the two computer operators, who usually brought sandwiches from home. These two now tried to point out to her that jobs like theirs were hard to come by. 'There are men who can't wait to step into our shoes, with all the unemployment,' Belinda said. But Kehinde had made her decision.

Her colleagues chose one lunch hour to give her a parting gift and to wish her farewell. Her immediate boss, Arthur, tried to tease her about her reasons for leaving. 'K must have been longing for her old man. You miss him don't you?' Even though Kehinde had worked with him for over ten years, Arthur never called her by her full name, making light of his failure to pronounce it correctly. Now she could see that he was poking fun at her. 'You're probably going home to have a baby, like your friend,' he continued.

'I'm going back to my country. What's wrong with that? I never intended to settle here permanently,' Kehinde countered, suppressing the knowledge that, apart from her immediate family, she had been away too long for her absence to matter to anyone. Arthur merely arched his brows and shrugged, a gesture which did little to hide his indifference. Kehinde was presented with a gold-plated carriage clock and a card which everybody had signed. She had already been replaced by a keen young white man, who was obviously popular with the female employees. She wondered momentarily how Moriammo would cope without her, on her return from maternity leave.

When Kehinde tried to telephone Albert to tell him what she had done, she found his line was out of order. Kehinde had forgotten one did not take communications for granted in Nigeria. She left a message instead with one of his cousins, and Albert rang back the following day. He was so angry he could barely speak, accusing Kehinde of being mad to contemplate resigning. 'I've already resigned,' Kehinde shouted back down the echoing line. He could at least speak to her politely, considering he was calling from a relative's sitting-room. This enraged Albert even more, that she should think they had anything to conceal from Egbueze and his wife. She had not even learned how to talk of relations and yet she was coming home. She should go back to her job, try again to sell the house, and wait until he sent for her. 'Don't you miss me at all, Albert?' she almost whimpered, and instantly felt like killing herself for such self-indulgence. 'You have to prepare properly for your departure,' Albert said with finality.

'I don't want to prepare properly,' Kehinde was close to tears. 'I want us to be together. I want to see the children. I miss you all. It's two years since you left, have you forgotten?'

Whatever Albert said was lost as the phone went dead, and Kehinde found herself staring blankly at the mouthpiece.

11 Arrival

Kehinde waited impatiently at the airport at Heathrow. You could always tell the Nigeria Airways check-in counter, as it was the noisiest and the most chaotic in the terminal. There was, in fact, a passenger queue, but only those who had no personal contacts behind the desk stayed on it. Why queue if you could use influence to go through first? After two hours of standing still while people came from behind and were accepted, Kehinde was becoming jittery. It was common knowledge that Nigeria Airways planes were usually overbooked. The woman behind her told her that it was the third successive day she had tried to get on a flight, even though she already had a boarding pass. 'But you've paid,' Kehinde cried.

'You think they don't know that? I have no money to bribe anybody, that's why I can't get on. If I spend everything here, what will I do when I get to Nigeria?'

Kehinde's eyes were as red as palm kernels. She had to get on that plane. Going back home with all her luggage and incurring the expense of another taxi was not worth thinking about.

'We have to go and see them.' Amaka, who had come with her husband to see her off, cut across her thoughts.

'But why, when we came on time? We were here three hours before take off. After that expensive ride, I have no money left with which to see anybody.'

'Yes, but it seems we're in Nigeria already. The British officials won't interfere, even with all the noise. They let us do it our way,' commented Oseloke. 'So our way it is.' He ripped his rain coat off and threw it at his wife, rolled up his shirt sleeves, gave

64

them a grin, and forced his way to the front, where he was swallowed by the hysterical mob.

Kehinde and Amaka smiled knowingly at each other. 'He has to make a drama out of everything,' said Amaka, as her husband came puffing back. Unceremoniously, he hauled Kehinde's biggest bag onto his head, shouting, 'Out of my way! Out of my way!' Kehinde, confounded, followed in the wake he was carving through the crowd. Oseloke dropped the bags on the weighing machine, and turned round. Kehinde and Amaka were right behind him, along with the woman who had been talking to them. With the air of a little lad whose favourite football team had just scored the winning goal, he snatched the tickets from the hands of the bemused women, and pushed them under the nose of the tired looking man at the counter. The air around them buzzed with the noise of other passengers shouting foul.

Oseloke pretended not to hear. He kept pushing the tickets at the man until he too protested, 'All right, all right, I can see them.'

It was then the man looked up. It was Tunde, Moriammo's husband. Kehinde stared into his eyes. She had completely forgotten that Tunde worked as a counter clerk for Nigeria Airways.

Tunde recovered first. 'So you dey go home now, enh Mrs Okolo? That good-o. You no even tell your friend, but I go tell her, sha. You for tell me before, I for done check you in long time.'

As he spoke, he lugged the rest of Kehinde's bags onto the machine. He pretended not to notice that they weighed over thirty kilos instead of the stipulated twenty. As he did not even ask for his hand to be oiled, the watching passengers must have concluded that Kehinde was a good friend of his. And, indeed, Tunde was very affable, seemingly relieved to see Kehinde going home to her husband. 'I'll see you later, to give you a message for my friend,' he called, as Kehinde and her companions moved away from the crowded counter. The woman who had checked in along with Kehinde knelt on the terminal floor and thanked Oseloke again and again.

When, much later, Kehinde saw Tunde looking for her to give her the message for Albert, she hid in the ladies' toilet. 'What do you want to talk to me about?' she wondered. 'Or do you want to gloat that you have succeeded in putting a wedge between Moriammo and me, by using baby Olumide to reawaken her duty as a Muslim woman? I am sure you'll be surprised by Moriammo's reaction when she learns that I left without telling her. Our friendship is deeper than you can ever imagine, Tunde.'

Kehinde hid behind a door in the ladies until Tunde left the departure lounge. She hoped that the plane would leave on time, but there was the usual engine trouble, and her anxiety mounted the longer they had to wait. She knew her sister Ifeyinwa and Albert would be waiting for her at the airport in Lagos. One tiresome announcement after another told them it would only take another hour. The hour seemed to extend itself indefinitely. Knowing there was nothing she could do about the situation, Kehinde slept. At 9.30 the following morning, eleven hours behind schedule, they departed.

The journey was uneventful, but by the time they landed in Lagos, relatives who had been waiting all day had gone home. At least they had arrived in daylight.

In fact, Albert was waiting, and despite his disapproval over the telephone, he seemed glad to see her. He looked more imposing than the London Albert, in flowing white lace *agbada* and matching skull cap. His skin was darker and glossier, and he exuded a new confidence. Women knew the country did this to their men. There was no doubt about it, Albert was thoroughly at home.

A note discreetly pressed into the palm of one of the men jostling each other to take possession of Kehinde's bags, and the young tough was transformed into the picture of servility and respect. Kehinde, impressed in spite of herself, allowed Albert to take over. It was a long time since she had had the luxury of being looked after. She had arrived keyed up and combative, ready to justify herself, but slipped effortlessly back into her old submissive rôle. Besides, there was something about Albert's new confidence which excited admiration, made him more attractive.

Their old Jaguar did not look old at all compared to the other cars on the Lagos road. Though Albert was a careful driver, Kehinde could detect strange sounds that had not been there before, as old bones creak under the still taut skin that holds them together.

When they were under way, Kehinde felt comfortable enough to ask after the children.

'They're fine. I saw them last Saturday and told them Mama is coming home, and they're waiting for you.' Knowing this would please her, Albert gave Kehinde a quick grin, revealing momentarily the old Albert. He had never been an openly demonstrative person, but in the last two years he had acquired a new layer of self-control and detachment.

'Something wrong?' Kehinde asked.

'No, nothing. Why you ask?'

'I don't know. I just feel . . .'

Albert did not help her out, concentrating on the traffic. Kehinde was impressed by what oil had done for Lagos. Beautiful wide roads, elegant individually designed houses, soaring fly-overs. It was almost like a developed country. Kehinde filled her lungs with hot tropical air and felt elated.

Perhaps Albert had been angry with her because he felt neglected, even though he had taken the decision that he would go back to Lagos ahead of her. She was to sell the house, and buy more things they would need in Lagos. Albert needed time to find accommodation for all of them. Maybe he had forgotten, and that was why he was sulking. Men! Sometimes they behave just like children. After all, their going home was his idea in the first place, urged on by his sisters.

She tried to bring the smile back to his face by asking, 'Aunt Selina and Aunt Mary, do they write you often?'

Albert took his eyes off the road and studied her, as if she were someone he had just met. Kehinde was not sure if the sigh that escaped him was of boredom or pity. He turned his attention once more to the road and replied as if he were addressing the streets that were unfolding before their eyes, 'Their generation don't like writing letters much. They are here in the south, visiting. We all came to the airport yesterday, but your plane did not arrive . . .'

'You mean they are all at home, in our house! I mean the bungalow you rented?' Kehinde asked, aghast.

'They are in the south to welcome you and to visit the children at their school. Where else do you want them to be?'

Kehinde had harboured the dream of their being alone together for a few days, now that the children were at school. She knew now that she had to nerve herself for a different scenario. Staying in the same house with Albert's sisters was more than she had bargained for.

Suddenly, without warning, they were plunged into a maelstrom of fumes, car horns, careering big yellow buses, minibuses packed to capacity and people: the heart of Lagos, Lagos Island-Eko. Kehinde, unaccustomed to the noise and chaos, was startled, but Albert picked his way adroitly through narrow side roads, cluttered with abandoned cars. They turned at last into a small but freshly tarred road, lined with colourful bungalows. This street was cleaner, though the smell of rotting rubbish coming from the open gutters was suffocating. Albert stopped finally in front of a neat bungalow painted pale blue and white. Two wide pieces of plank had been nailed together to form a bridge over the gutter which smelt so bad that Kehinde wanted to throw up.

A girl ran out to meet them. 'Welcome, Madam, welcome, sah,' she greeted, as she pulled the bags out of the boot. Kehinde was manoeuvring herself out of the car when her attention was diverted to the main door of the house. She was dumbstruck at the sight in front of her. A very beautiful, sophisticated, young, pregnant woman, with a baby on her left hip, stood in the doorway, wearing the same white lace material as Albert. Her hair, drawn back and plaited in the latest upside-down-basket style, made her face look narrower, so that her swollen belly was like a badge of womanhood in contrast to her leanness. She scrutinised Kehinde insolently, smiling in a mild and unenthusiastic way. She did not attempt to come and help with the unpacking. Kehinde took it all in, like a film in slow motion.

'Grace! Grace, make you careful with those cases,' Albert said sharply, appearing unaware of the drama about to be enacted.

'Yes sah!' the encumbered Grace called over her shoulder, as she staggered across the wooden bridge with Kehinde's case on her head.

Just then, Kehinde was distracted by the arrival of Ifeyinwa, shouting for joy and almost dancing her welcome. A couple of her numerous children followed in her wake, and between the three of them, they almost lifted her bodily from the ground. She found herself for the first time crying tears of joy, mixed with relief at receiving a genuine welcome. By now, almost half the street had gathered to watch and to welcome her. People she had never met were asking her how England was.

Ifeyinwa took control. She ushered her sister inside the large and fashionably decorated living room, tastefully enchanced by the furniture Kehinde had sent home in a separate container after Albert had left London. A part of their old life was there in that room and Kehinde felt a surge of reassurance at the familiarity of it.

Ifeyinwa, who used to be a quiet women, was talking incessantly. She was thinner than Kehinde remembered, certainly compared with Kehinde's plumpness. She exuded anxiety, tying and retying her top *lappa* in agitation. She seemed bent on protecting her, even from people who came in to say she was welcome.

Where was Albert, who should be showing her around, taking her to their room? Instead, she felt Ifeyinwa pulling her. 'We're coming,' she told a neighbour who wanted to know if Kehinde had, by sheer accident, met her sons who were studying somewhere in the East End of London. 'I have to take her to her room. You can ask her later. After all, you're neighbours now,' Ifeyinwa explained. She pulled Kehinde more determinedly, so she had no choice but to follow.

Ifeyinwa led her to her room. It was clean, simply and neatly furnished with one of the three single beds she had bought in London. Where was the king size bed on which she and Albert had spent a fortune in Harrods? Albert had said in his letter that

69

everything had arrived in good condition. She had never had a separate room from her husband all their married life.

'Little Mother, Ifi, call Albert for me. Where is he?' Kehinde besought her sister.

Ifeyinwa opened her eyes in horror. 'Sh . . . sh . . . sh, not so loud! Don't call your husband by his name here-o. We hear you do it over there in the land of white people. There, people don't have respect for anybody. People call each other by the name their parents gave them, however big the person. We don't do it here-o. Please Kehinde, don't-o.'

Kehinde heard herself laughing mirthlessly. 'What are you talking about? I said I wanted Albert. Where is he?' She made her way towards the door, but Ifeyinwa restrained her.

'Where are you going? Come back in, just come back. You will see Joshua's father later. Just come first.' Her eyes were red and her voice was agitated. 'Where do you think you are? This is Nigeria, you know.'

'I know that, that's what everybody says. "This is Nigeria, this is Nigeria," as if the country were not part of this world.'

'Sit down, baby sister. Do sit down. You left home a very long time ago. Here, men move together, you know. We women stick together too.'

'Educate me, please, have I not just got married to Albert and you are now going to tell me what marriage is all about. Where is he, anyway?'

'He knows I'm here and won't barge in like that. He's a cultured man. You must stop calling him by his given name. His sisters are in the front room and so are many of his friends and neighbours to welcome you. You are not going out there shouting his given name as if he is your houseboy; as if you circumcised him. What a cheek! What do you want him for anyway? He'll see you bye and bye. Just get dressed, get ready to go and see those who have been waiting to greet you.'

Kehinde looked around her once more. 'This is not our room, surely?'

'Our room? This is your room. I chose it for you. Next to Joshua's father's own, this is the best one, even better than Rike's own. She has to share hers with her maid and her baby, and she is next to the room kept for your husband's sisters, who can be very noisy during their visits. You're lucky. Joshua's father allowed me a free hand. He is cultured, that husband of yours.'

'You talk about my husband as if he's a stranger to me. We married seventeen years ago and I should be telling you about him.'

'That's one of the things you must learn. Stop calling him "my" husband. You must learn to say "our". He is Rike's husband too, you know. You saw her, that shameless one with a pregnancy in her belly and a baby on her hips. Honestly, "these their acadas" just jump on any been-to man, so that they can claim their husbands studied overseas . . .' She trailed on, flailing those annoying arms, and not even standing still. She stopped for breath suddenly, gasping.

Kehinde made as if to stand up, but she pulled her down again. 'Sit down and calm yourself.'

'I am sitting down. I am calm. You are the one who has been walking up and down like . . . like . . . oh Ifi, I don't know like what. Are you trying to tell me that Albert's got another wife, and that he is the father of the baby that woman was carrying?'

Ifeyinwa nodded, mutely, tears rolling down her face. 'Her name is Rike. She actually pushed herself on Joshua's father. When I heard she'd had a baby boy, I knew Albert would marry her. Few men would say no to such an educated woman once she'd had a man-child for them. His sisters would not have allowed it, and you yourself wouldn't let Joshua's father throw away a man-child, would you? Then, before we could bat an eyelid, she was carrying another one. But I thank your *chi*, that has made you into such a strong woman, that at least you are the mother of Joshua and Bimpe. This one, with all her bottom power and all her acada, cannot take that from you. This is nothing that has not been seen or heard of before. It happens all the time. My husband has two other wives and we all live in two rooms. At least here you have a whole house, and Albert is in a good job. That one is a big teacher at the university.'

Kehinde was kneading one of the pillows she'd taken absent-

71

mindedly from the bed. She stared at her sister. She could now
see why the two of them had been left alone – so that Ifeyinwa
could prevent her from going out and making a fool of herself.
Her eyes were red, but there were no tears. Her voice, when she
eventually found it, was calm, but came from a distance. 'So,
Albert married her because she had a baby boy for him, enh?'

The past rolled itself out like a film in Kehinde's mind. Albert
had insisted they could not keep the baby because they could not
afford it, and yet it too had been a man-child. Was that what her
dead parents were trying to warn her in the dream she had had
in the hospital? But as she looked at her sister, she knew she
could not share this pain with her. Kehinde knew her reaction
would be to tell her that God was punishing her for committing
such an abomination. Possibly Albert was counting on that too.
Meanwhile, Ifeyinwa was crying for both of them. She looked at
her sister again and their eyes met. Kehinde tried to imagine the
anguish and helplessness she must have endured these last
months, not knowing how to break the news to her. Something
inside her advised caution, to act coolly and thank God and her
culture for her sister's support.

A loud knock coupled with loud laughter at the door told them
that their time alone together was over and the play-acting was
to begin. A big woman burst in, a typical successful Nigerian
businesswoman, known locally as 'tick madam'. Not waiting to
be invited, she entered with a breezy confidence that indicated
unmistakably that the house was hers. She was Aunt Selina, the
eldest of the Okolo family, whom Kehinde remembered from her
engagement to Albert as a thin woman who had just lost her
husband, and had been left with two children of her husband's
by another woman to look after. She had no child of her own.
Her other relatives, Aunt Mary and the other brother Nicholas,
had stood by her, while she quickly sold off all her husband's
property and went to stay in the north, away from the harassment
of her in-laws. The money had helped to educate Nicholas and
paid her passage when Albert sent for her, and her bride price.
One could never say to such a woman, 'Why don't you wait until
I say come in?' She was now known as Mama Kaduna and was

the mother of them all. Kehinde had thought at one time that when they returned to Nigeria, they would be above all that, and people like Mama Kaduna and Aunt Mary would be kept in their places. Now she knew she had been wrong. They were stronger than she was.

She held Kehinde in a bear hug. 'Let me look at you. Let's just look at you. Olisa, thank you for bringing them all home. Look at that tiny girl that a rat would eat and still want some more. Look at her. Has she not grown into a mature woman? Hold your head up! Your chin must always be up. Or don't you know who you are? You are the senior wife of a successful Nigerian man, the first wife of the first son of our father, Okolo. Olisa, give him peace where he is now, making merry with his age-mates. Our dead father loved beautiful people, and you are beautiful now, my daughter. So cool and round.' As she spoke, she shot Ifeyinwa a knowing look, as if to emphasise her deficiencies. Ifeyinwa was even thinner than when she was young, not fashionably so, but worn down by poverty. Ignoring the malice, Ifeyinwa merely responded, 'Yes Ma, you're right.'

Mama Kaduna turned again to Kehinde for a concluding appraisal: 'Ah London suited you, but here will suit you even better,' she said, as she swept into the sitting room. She called back over her shoulder, 'There are people here wanting to greet you, don't keep them waiting.'

When Mama Kaduma was out of earshot, Kehinde asked breathlessly, 'Do Joshua and Bimpe know?'

'Of course they know. I told Bimpe not to mention it to you in her letters. She is full of understanding, that girl of ours. I told her it would probably shock you, and that it is very unwise for people living alone to suffer such shocks. It is better to break it to you this way, don't you think? I have noticed that recently, she has accepted Rike too, and understands why Albert had to marry her. She knew her father was lonely, and besides, Rike has been a real little mother to them. She visits them most Saturdays and makes sure they have everything they need. Let's face it, she's been helping you to look after your family, since you could not have been in two places at once.'

73

'But why didn't Albert give me even a hint that this was the way of life he wanted?'

'What rubbish you talk. Men don't say such things. It's like asking why a man did not tell his wife before taking a mistress. But he must have left hints, you must have seen it in his behaviour. You were probably too sure of your position to notice, and too busy giving him orders. Why do you think he was not keen on your returning immediately?'

'That was my fault. I wasn't quite sure I wanted to come back just then, and of course there was the house to be sold . . .'

'Ah, you see what I mean. You forgot it was Lagos he was returning to. There are many ways of catching a fish, and Rike used the cleverest. She met Albert when he was low, with neither job nor accommodation, and presented herself as a ministering angel, even taking him to her church. She became so enmeshed in his life that when the children returned, Joshua thought she was one of their aunties. And when he found out, he soon became reconciled to it.'

'But what did he say to his father?'

'To his father? What could he say? This is Nigeria; you don't talk to your father anyhow.'

'Oh my God, why have I been so blind? How can Albert have changed so fast?'

'I tell you, Rike is a clever African woman, in spite of her book knowledge. But don't worry, you'll soon get used to it, and then you'll be wondering why you were worried in the first place. Albert is a good, hard working man. Just relax and enjoy your life.'

Kehinde was too overwhelmed by her sister's news to count how many faces she saw that night, of old friends she had forgotten, people who had been children when she left and were now grown men and women, with families of their own. Her only emotion was one of consternation at how much had changed, but she viewed it all with detachment. That first night reminded her of her first visit to Ibusa, long, long ago, when she was a child. She felt as lost now as she had felt then. Even the way people talked had changed, showing a whole range of jokes and expressions which meant nothing whatever to her.

On the faces of some of the women, however, she could clearly read a combination of helplessness and sympathy. To the one or two who expressed themselves verbally, Ifeyinwa replied: 'But now Joshua has a brother, to back him in a fight. Ogochukwu will always be there to support him from the rear,' and all agreed that there was nothing as heartrending as a single male defending his father's compound. Though nobody said it directly, the consensus obviously was that Kehinde should take things as she found them.

She caught sight of Albert once or twice, at the centre of proceedings, ordering drinks, seeing to the music, and accepting compliments on behalf of his senior wife. He was remote and distant, as though tradition had put a wedge between them, just as it had apparently between him and Joshua, or Joshua would have protested. He must have learned quickly that here a father was to be respected. Kehinde's heart went out to her children for the adjustments they had had to make.

It was a long time before Kehinde was allowed to leave the party, and she was exhausted. She fell at once into a deep sleep, visited by fragments of the past, as if, in her depleted state, her spirit was seeking solace in its own beginnings.

12 Origins

It was just before the rainy season, when we had the long school holidays. Since I didn't have to go to school, I used to go to market with Aunt Nnebogo instead. I had got up early to go and have my bath, when Olu, one of the landlord's children, opened the door of the yard to allow a pair of strangers to enter.

'These visitors are for your Mama, and they have a car!' she hissed at me excitedly. We left the visitors by the door of our room, and she and I ran outside to see the car. It was big and black, and it sat on the ground like a duck sheltering chicks under its wings. We ran around it, fingering its protruberances admiringly. We had never seen a car that close before. Suddenly I remembered I was wrapped only in a towel, and I dashed back into the yard before Mama could catch me.

Aunt Nnebogo was standing talking to the two strange men and I stopped in my tracks. Not knowing what else to say, I burst out, 'I am Kehinde.' The older of the men laughed and said, 'We know who you are. Hurry up and have your bath, we must get to Ibusa today, and we must leave before it gets too hot.' He obviously noticed the expression on my face, as he went on to explain: 'Your father sent us a message from Sokoto, asking us to take you home. Your sister wants to see you before she gets married.' Turning to Mama, he said, 'Her age-mates will teach her what's expected. She's a war baby, isn't she?'

I did not know what an age-mate was, but I knew when I was born: 20 August 1943, and I told him so.

'Oh, not yet twelve? You coast girls look so big, or is it your

Aunty's care? Your age group is the year day turned into midnight.'

Mama cut us short. 'Kehinde, hurry now, go and bath,' she commanded. 'There is a long journey ahead of you.' While I bathed, she packed my things into a *shuku*, while my school books went into a raffia bag. I didn't stop to wonder at this, nor did I notice my aunt's sadness. I was too excited at the thought of meeting my father, and brothers and sisters, and getting some answers to my questions.

By the door, Mama hugged me and said, 'Take care of yourself. Greet your father for me.' It was then I noticed she had tears in her eyes, but I was already climbing into the back seat of the car, swollen with pride that Olu was watching me enviously. The older man got into the driving seat and said good-bye to Mama, promising to bring her a girl when he returned from the village. Once again, I did not stop to question why Mama needed another girl to live with her, when she had me. I was mesmerised by the interior of the car, its smell and the feel of the upholstery. I waved to Olu like a queen as we manoeuvred our way out of the street and onto the highway.

In no time, it seemed, the houses and streets had given way to countryside. The thick, green vegetation, which was all I could see from the car window, became monotonous, and I must have fallen asleep. I woke when we reached the outskirts of Benin, a blur of dusty-rooved houses waiting to be washed by the rain. The older man, who said he was my uncle, bought me a packet of plantain chips, which I was unable to eat. I was still holding them when we arrived in Ibusa nearly two hours later.

There was a big house, painted yellow, with people rushing out from all directions. They snatched my basket and raffia bag from the men who had brought me, thanking the one who said he was my uncle. He smiled at me, and said good-bye. Then he drove away.

In the sea of faces, that of one young girl stood out. She was slimmer and older than I was, otherwise I might have thought she was my twin – my living Taiwo. She stepped forward and hugged me, saying, 'My baby sister, I could pick you out even in a crowded market. Welcome. I am your big sister, Ifeyinwa.'

'You haven't seen her before, then?' asked an old lady, who was smiling at me and holding my wooden Taiwo. Her face was crisscrossed with many smiling wrinkles.

'Never. They sent her away when she was born. Then papa was transferred to Sokoto, and we never saw her again.'

The old woman smiled, as if all the tiny fine wrinkles on her face were saying 'Don't cry, don't cry,' to my sister. Aloud she said, 'But she is alive and well. Look at her, how plump. Look at her skin, how smooth and shiny. Look at her eyes, clear enough to stare at the stars. Wipe your eyes, my daughter. There's nothing like having a sister of one's own to lend balance to life. When you live in your husband's house, you will soon stop growing, and she will catch up with you. Then you will be women and sisters, and your friendship will be sweeter than honey.'

Involuntarily, my body shook. One thing was very clear, Mama Nnebogo was not my mother, but where my mother was I did not know. Ifeyinwa, my sister, led me into the house to a room where a huge dark man was sitting on a leather chair, drinking beer with another man. This man was equally dark but wiry, with tobacco-stained teeth. The huge man bellowed, 'Come here and say hello to your father. Is it really you, my daughter? Children grow so fast.' He turned to the other man and introduced me.

'This is Elege's last surviving baby. The other one went with the mother.'

'So, you have not seen her for a long time?'

'No, Sokoto is too far. I was transferred after her birth. Come, come and greet your father,' he addressed me again.

'Are you my real father?' I asked, wondering why I had not been allowed to stay with the rest of my family.

They laughed, and my father's friend exclaimed, 'Children from the coast! They answer questions with question.'

I found myself sitting on my father's lap, while he introduced many other children, both older and younger, as my brothers and sisters. Finally, he introduced me to a tall, pale woman, so pale she looked like a woman of mixed blood. She had cool green eyes that did not smile. When my father talked to her, she looked over the heads of the men sitting. 'This is your mother now,' Father said.

'How?' I cried. 'How many mothers do I have?'

They laughed again, but the man sitting by my father sensed my confusion and the fact that I did not like their laughing at me. He said, 'Onuorah, explain to her. Children in Lagos learn only from books, you know. That is why it is important to bring them home once in a while so that they can learn from life as well.'

Father nodded, and began: 'That lady is your mother because she is my wife. Your own mother died when you were born.'

He stopped talking when he saw the shock in my eyes. Yet I was not too shocked, for somehow I had always linked my mother with my Taiwo, who was dead. I lost interest in the rest of the story of my life. I had longed for this mysterious woman, but now that I knew that she was no more, I suddenly wanted to be with the woman I had thought was my mother for so long. I wondered when they would take me back to her.

My father spoke again: 'In our culture, few people are raised by their real parents. Your real mother carries you for nine months, but think of those who carry all our troubles, who feed us, who comfort us as we grow up. Those women are our mothers too. The lady who has looked after you from birth did it because she felt you were her child. She is my younger sister, yet she is your mother too. And that lady there,' pointing to the old lady with all the smiling lines on her face, 'is our big mother, because she is my older sister. Ifeyinwa is your sister, but you can even call her your little mother.'

'But the educated people call their little mothers "seesita"!' laughed our big mother, who was supervising one of my innumerable brothers as he pounded yam.

One of the men who were now drinking with father, laughed and said, 'Mother, I didn't know you knew Grammar.'

'I'm not deaf. I can hear when people speak English words

like "I culudu", "goo'mony", "seesita", "buloder" and more.'
Everybody laughed again at big mother's jokes about the English
language. My brother Mark, who was fifteen and could contrib-
ute to the adults' discussion because, Ifeyinwa told me, he was
at King's College, added: 'And by English standard, we are not
Kehinde's real brothers and sisters because our mothers are
different even though we have the same father.'

The men murmured and one of them exclaimed, 'Have you
ever heard such rubbish? Children of the same father calling
each other "half". No wonder the white people's country is a
place of everybody for himself.' They all laughed again. I had
never heard so much laughter. And I was still confused. I did
not see why Aunt Nnebogo should have taken me away from my
brothers and sisters, whether they were half or full. I would have
liked to have grown up among them, familiar and close as they
were. I had to watch what I said because I did not want them to
laugh at me, but I wanted to protest, to say that when I grow
up, I am going to be like the white people. I will look after my
own only, since for over eleven years I did not know of my
family's existence. But Ifeyinwa caught my eye and shook her
head. So I smiled instead, and joined in the laughter. My big
mother saw my face and remarked, 'Doesn't our daughter have
the same look as Onuorah?' For the first time, my father's
beautiful wife, the one with green eyes and pale skin, turned from
the soup she was stirring on the open fire and looked at me. She
did not smile and she did not speak.

Ifeyinwa and I quickly became very close. We shared a room
with other cousins and sisters, and I slept next to her on the
large mattress on the floor. It was more comfortable than the
mat I slept on in Lagos at Aunty Nnebogo's place. Ifeyinwa
showed me the kind of love and closeness I had never before
experienced. 'Why didn't they let me stay with you all this time?'
I asked her one night. In a low voice, so as not to wake the
others, she said: 'They believed you ate your sister in our
mother's tummy. The doctors told our mother to take something
to purge you out, because if not she would die, but she said she
wanted you to taste life. Since you carried your *chi* and that of

80

Taiwo, letting you die would mean killing two people. When she died giving birth to you, she gave you her *chi* also. Everybody was frightened of looking after such a child. That sad one with snake eyes refused to have you, in case you brought bad luck to her children. But Aunt Nnebogo took you, and from what we heard, you brought her good luck instead of bad. But recently she wrote that you kept asking for your mother, and that you did not accept her any more. If they had told you the truth at the very beginning, you would have known that you had no real mother and would have taken her as the mother you lost. But they kept it a secret and of course you became curious. I think now they plan to send you to a boarding school. Lucky girl! I am not as clever as you are because I had to do a great deal of housework to help the green-eyed one and her innumerable babies. The good thing is that my husband's work is in Lagos, and your school is just outside Lagos, so during holidays, you can come and stay with me or with Aunty Nnebogo. But the family house in Sokoto! Pooh, it's like a zoo. Everybody having children all the time. You wouldn't like to stay there.'

'You don't like our father's wife very much, do you sister Ifeyinwa?'

'How can you like a woman who never smiles, simply because she is beautiful and has many children? Don't worry, after your schooling, in just a few years time, you'll get a husband who loves you, and then you'll start your own family. You will marry well because of the education father is preparing for you.'

That night, I cried for the mother I did not know. Ifeyinwa knew who I was crying for, and held me tightly in the dark, crying too. Then we went to sleep.

My sister Ifeyinwa was dark and slim. She already had tiny breasts like my big friend Malechi in Macaullum Street. I wanted breasts too. Sometimes I would tie lemons in my school dress, pretending, but would quickly let them roll down when I knew that someone was staring at me.

We girls had to go to the stream every morning, and one day, I asked Ifeyinwa how long it would be before I had my own breasts. My sister answered all my questions patiently. She only became impatient if I refused to do what she said.

'When you grow older,' she said, counting with her fingers. 'Within a year or two, you'll start having breasts and then you will bleed. And then you'll be ready for marriage.'

'When will all that be?'

'In a few years time, when the time comes.'

'Why will I bleed?'

'You will bleed so you can have children, but you must not announce it to everybody, because it is your secret. And you must keep yourself clean.'

'Why does the blood smell?'

'Oh oooo, *Ojugo*! You are going to crowd me out of this world with so many questions.'

A few weeks later we all wore white cloth and went to the market to celebrate our mother's life. I had *ehulu* in my hair, and around my neck and wrists. Ifeyinwa, being the *adah*, our mother's eldest daughter, danced with each group in turn, my brothers and myself trailing behind her. My mother was acknowledged to be a woman with a life worth celebrating, a mother of seven boys and two girls. My father made sure that each of us had professional praise singers. A group of dancers from Ifeyinwa's new family performed so many acrobatic feats that sometimes I forgot I was one of the mourners, and should be stepping lightly to the music made by my praise singers, instead of staring at them.

Big mother taught me how to shake the black horse tail I was carrying, and to take two steps forward and one backward, while answering, 'Eh, eh, onmu, onmu' to the praises of my name. The singers called: 'Who has the *chi* of three great women in her?' and I responded, 'Onmu, it is me.' 'Who came as two seeds in one?' 'Onmu, eh, eh, eh.' I was fascinated by the men with powerful arms beating the drums, which were carried by younger men. As they drummed, we raised our black horse tails in the air and stepped backwards and forwards. Our hands went up and down with the rhythm of the drums.

In the marketplace a circle was formed for us to dance.

Ifeyinwa and I, our mother's only daughters, danced first. My sister's body was like rubber, coiling and uncoiling as if it were boneless, while her arms, with two heavy horse tails in her hands, rose and fell as she danced. When the boys danced, they stamped heavily, raising dust and jumping, pointing their horse tails into the air as if they were going to shoot the heavens. We girls were encouraged to carry ours in a more graceful way.

After the dancing, we took a huge cow as a gift to my mother's people, to thank them for giving us our mother. They gave us little gifts of yams and kolanuts, and advised us that if we felt badly treated in our father's house, we could always come back to our mother's compound. More women were introduced to us as mothers again, but by this point I was distracted by the acrobatic dancers and not listening very much. My sister and my big brother, who was going to university that year, however, were listening attentively.

Two weeks later, Ifeyinwa's husband's people came to take her away. She left at night, all of us singing her praises and carrying hurricane lamps to light her to her new home. Ifeyinwa cried throughout the ceremony, in which our father prayed for her happiness.

After she left, I stayed another four days, but it was no longer fun, and I missed Ifeyinwa. On the fourth day, they put me on a bus that was taking some students to the same convent school to which I was going. I did not miss my father. He had so many people to love that I felt insignificant.

My brothers helped me to take my few possessions to the bus garage. I never knew my brothers very well, as I did not grow up with them, and I felt they were like gods, only to be spoken to on rare and important occasions. Our big mother came with us, and was full of advice and prayers. She said I should write to her often, but I am ashamed to say I never wrote, because she could not read, which meant that anything I said to her would be common knowledge.

In the convent outside Lagos I made new friends, who became more important to me than my family. Our people do not write letters much, preferring to see you face to face. Since I did not hear from my family in Sokoto nor the one in Ibusa, my new life crowded them out.

But my sister Ifi kept coming, trying to make up for the time we had lost as children. I could tell that her life was not easy. We both cried the day she came to tell me that Aunt Nnebogo had died. I told our Reverend Father, and the sisters at the convent encouraged me to mourn for her like my real mother. I wished I could have seen her before she died, but she left Lagos for Kaduna soon after I left her house. Maybe she missed me, but I had no way of knowing. We said a mass for her soul. After that, my life became wound around my books, getting qualified and leaving the convent to get married.

Albert came one day to see a neighbour's daughter, and we discovered that we were both from Ibusa. He was still at Eko Boys High School. Our friendship developed as my sister Ifeyinwa became more and more distant with the births of her babies. When she told me her husband had married another woman, I felt as if I wanted to erase them all from my mind. Albert's attitude was that polygamy was degrading for women, which he based on his own experience with his father's two wives. I therefore thought we were of the same mind on the matter.

I went to visit Ifeyinwa once during the Easter holidays, and what I saw of the way they lived put me off large families and polygamy for ever. After the near clinical cleanliness of the convent, I found even a few days there chaotic and lacking in privacy. I returned to school before anybody else, and the nuns laughed. After that, I would have lost touch with my past, except that Ifi kept coming, and was not offended at my shunning her way of life.

When it became clear that Albert was coming to England, he asked me to marry him, and I happily agreed. I thought we would escape for ever the way of life our parents had, and Ifi kept reminding me, 'Did I not tell you that you would marry well?'

13   *School Visit*

It was the third day since Kehinde had arrived from London, and she still had not been alone in the same room with Albert, who was always surrounded by friends and relatives. Frequently she thought she caught him trying to steal a glance at her, his eyes red-rimmed and yearning, but by the time he had finished with the relatives, she was already in bed.

On the third night, Kehinde woke to feel his hands moving around her body. She had rehearsed many things to say when Albert finally came to her, but she had not bargained for the unexpectedness. Instead of the cool detachment she had planned, she asked abruptly, 'What do you want with me, Alby?'

He was taken aback, and answered in a low voice, 'You must realise this is Nigeria. Things are different here.' 'So I see. You don't need me now. I wish to God you'd had the guts to tell me all this before I resigned my job in England.'

'Did I not try to stop you, and did you listen?'

Kehinde got up, pushed Albert away from her and put on the light, grateful that for once the electricity had not been cut off. The single room was illuminated by a lone light bulb dangling from a thin cable wire, with a sickly blue shade made of transparent paper. Kehinde suspected, despite Ifeyinwa's protestations, that the room had been used by Joshua and Bimpe, and had been hurriedly prepared for her. She was supposed to be grateful even for that. 'Why have you been avoiding me, Alby?' she asked.

'Avoiding you? Don't be ridiculous. Don't you see how busy life is here? Tomorrow is Saturday, and we will go and see

Joshua and Bimpe in their school.' Kehinde noticed that Albert was already standing up, and had not protested at her putting on the light. Moriammo's warning was ringing in her mind: 'Nigeria na man's country. Dem get plenty, plenty women wey dey chase after dem, sha.' Albert was still talking. 'Next week, we'll start looking for a job for you. Every educated woman works here.'

'I've always worked, so what's new?'

'It is different here. Here it is a must for women.'

'I know that. This is Africa, where women do all the work. I am not going to depend on you. I am going to work to keep myself.'

'I know you're angry. But look back, Kehinde. My father had two wives, yours had three, so what sin did I commit that is so abominable?' Albert's voice grated.

'Did they marry in church? We had a church wedding, or have you forgotten? All those promises, don't they mean anything to you?'

'Everbody does that for immigration purposes, and anyway, Rike became pregnant.' His voice was rising as he allowed himself to be provoked. Now Kehinde was really interested. She wanted to know how within twenty-four months he could have fathered a son and have another on the way, how he could actually take another wife into the house he knew she would come to.

'So she became pregnant and you of course have never made a woman pregnant before. Congratulations, man-child's father!'

'You don't understand. That child Ogochukwu was born under a lucky star. A *woli* told me about him before he was born. As soon as I accepted his mother and allowed her to become my wife, I got this well-paying job. The *woli* told me that the child will bring so much luck to all of us that we won't know what came over us.' He came nearer to Kehinde, who moved towards the window, facing Albert squarely, as she listened to his story as if it were a midnight fable. 'I . . . I remember that man-child we lost. Well, I did not wish the same to happen again. My sisters have seen Rike with me. And Kehinde, she's not bad, you

86

know. She's very respectful, and will regard you as her mother, you'll see. You said you did not wish to go through the pain of another pregnancy. Well, she's young. She's keeping a good job at the university while coping with the births of her babies . . .'

Kehinde did not believe what she was hearing. 'This was not what we planned. We couldn't keep the baby because we had no money. Only a few months later, a prophet convinces you you are going to have a messiah. Oh Albert, what happened to you . . .' She stopped herself before she could weaken. She could tell that the prophet must have been from Rike's church. In England, Albert only went to church to get Joshua and Bimpe into a Catholic school. The Albert she knew was gone. If Rike was a member of a charismatic church, and if Albert had joined it, she knew she would be treading on very slippery ground. In no time at all, they would start seeing visions about her having bad feelings towards Rike, and they would be right. For a moment she felt she would be crushed by the enormity of what she faced. But she was still the mother of Joshua and Bimpe, and she must not allow herself to sink.

Kehinde was not quite sure when a troubled sleep overcame her, but she stayed awake for a long time after Albert left. Presently she heard the noises of morning coming from all the rooms. Rike in her rich cultured voice was telling her maid off. Her child was crying. Kehinde got up reluctantly, her body stiff. She had a feeling of wanting to die. This was supposed to be her family, and it was getting on perfectly well without her. Nobody had bothered to call her. They must have heard the argument with Albert during the night. He had tried to lower his voice, but she had been hurting so much that she had not cared who was listening. There was no privacy here. She smiled wryly. 'The family will be going to see our children tomorrow. You'd better come, they have been expecting you,' Albert had said when leaving her room. '*My* children now "our" children,' thought Kehinde, eyeing the presents she had brought for them. Their needs were now catered for by Rike and Mama Kaduna. But Kehinde determined she would go; after all, they were her children, they could not have changed that much. She dressed and went to join the rest of the household. Parcels of food were being stacked in the boot of the car, as if they were preparing to visit a refugee camp.

Kehinde made to sit in the front seat of the Jaguar, as she had done in London, daring Rike to challenge her right to sit next to Albert. Instead, Mama Kaduna's boisterous laughter halted her. She knew from the tone of the laughter that something was wrong. It was playful yet full of chagrin. She looked at the people standing around, but they simply looked away, or stared at the dusty road.

'My wife, I am coming too,' said Mama Kaduna, in a dangerously low voice. Kehinde was too new to hear the warning. 'Oh yes, Ma, I know,' she said as she sat down. Albert's face was impassive, but Mama Kaduna let forth a torrent of scorn and abuse.

'I say, I am coming with you. What is wrong with you? Do you think I came all the way from Kaduna just to welcome you? I came to see how the children are doing. So, who do you think you are? Don't you see your mate, Rike? Don't you see her sitting at the back with her maid and baby. When we, the relatives of the head of the family are here, we take the place of honour by our Albert. When you visit your brother's houses, the same honour will be accorded you. So, go to the back and let us move on.'

Kehinde almost died of shame. She saw that even the maid, Grace, was covering her mouth in an attempt not to laugh. Only young brides with poor training made such mistakes. Kehinde collected herself and forced herself to apologise. 'Yes, sorry, Aunty Selina. Been away too long. No offence.' Albert pretended not to hear, and Mama Kaduna did not bother to accept the apology. Kehinde squeezed into the back of the car with Rike, her baby and the maid. Albert put a Nigerian hit on the stereo, but Mama Kaduna talked above the music. Once or twice, Albert caught Kehinde's eye in the mirror, but looked away quickly, so the others would not notice. Kehinde knew that in his heart of hearts he was not enjoying all this.

Albert had wanted to come back to Nigeria of his youth, but

that Nigeria no longer existed, where people like his father had been happy to work as washermen, boat cleaners or wood carriers, and the women of the family did not go to school. That Nigeria was a nostalgic dream. He wondered what Kehinde would do now, for he was not blind to her difficulties. He consoled himself that she would soon settle down once she had a job.

'Our husband drives so carefully,' Rike, who did not miss a thing, said casually.

Our husband? oh yes, our husband. Albert was now 'our husband', or 'Joshua's father', as Ifeyinwa had pointed out the day of her arrival. Kehinde saw that he was trying to do three things at the same time – listen to the car radio, follow his sister's flow of words, and steer safely in the thick Lagos traffic.

Kehinde was lost in reminiscence. She saw herself in her fur coat, her crossed legs, not bothering to talk to Alby, listening to the music as he stole furtive glances at her to see if she was in the mood to talk. She would pretend not to see him, and he would glance again and maybe give a dry cough. Then she would say, 'What is it Alby?' They say that women talk a lot, but many years with Albert had taught her that she reached him more by being silent, and she had perfected this art, letting him talk while she half-listened.

Here women were supposed to stick together and a wife to give her husband room enough to be a man. This was not new to her so why was she finding it so difficult to accept? She felt she was being cheated, undervalued. She looked at Albert's young wife, a much more educated woman, bowing down to tradition. But through it, she had acquired a home and a big extended family for her children to belong to. In spite of her doctorate, she had got herself hooked to a man eighteen years her senior, with a wife and two children in England. Kehinde knew she did not stand a chance against Rike, with her Lagos sophistication. They were not playing by the same rules.

'I always like this part of Lagos. It has less traffic and the houses are so beautiful and well kept. Don't you think the streets

89

look beautiful, enh Mummy?' asked Rike. Kehinde, absorbed in her thoughts, did not hear.

'Kehinde, daughter of Nwabueze, are you still here with us?' came the explosive and impatient voice of Mama Kaduna. 'Your mate is talking to you.'

Kehinde woke up and again apologised. 'I beg-ooo, my mind just dey wander about. I am sorry, what were you saying?' Everybody laughed, but Rike did not repeat the question. It looked as if everybody was bent on exposing her. She shrugged her shoulders, turned her attention to the landscape and did not bother about those around her.

Mama Kaduna went on with her running commentary, from exactly where she had left off. Albert decided to drown his sister's voice by whistling softly to the music, but she did not mind if people were listening to her or not. She went on talking.

The car made a sharp turn onto a pebble covered road, edged by thick bushes and trees. At the end of the road, squatting right in the middle like an elephant urinating, stood the school, a huge ornate monstrosity. A flagpole on the roof proudly carried the green and white national flag. In front of the house, cars of all shapes and in different stages of disintegration were parked, while families, with members of all ages – from great grand-parents to babies – were coming and going, dressed as if for Christmas.

'This is the school,' Albert announced.

The school caretaker knew Mama Kaduna and welcomed her effusively, asking how she was, how her journey from the land of the Hausa people was, and hoping and praying to Allah that the family she left at home were all well. Mama Kaduna was asking the same questions of the man. At length, Grace, who knew from long practice when the greeting was waning, dashed to the car boot and brought the silver coated bowl which was packed with food stuffs, from kolanuts to chunks of meat, from fried snails to *akara*. Perched on top of this was a special parcel wrapped in newspaper. Mama Kaduna took this parcel and gave it to the caretaker. The man bowed as much as his short legs allowed him, but bowed an inch deeper when he saw Albert getting leisurely out of the car. He put the parcel inside his shirt and ran ahead to usher the visitors into the house. They were shown to a cool room, with comfortable chairs arranged along the white-washed walls. Through a door onto the compound, Kehinde could see bright little bungalows around an open field, with young people in starched white uniforms dashing to and fro. From the front, one would never have guessed that the compound was so large, with open verandas edged with palms and banana trees. Kehinde was happy to find her children in such an environment. Her happiness increased when Joshua and Bimpe appeared, tall, healthy and behaving like respectful Nigerian children. At least for them, the move had been a good one. If they seemed a little restrained towards her, she put it down to the presence of so many adults, and looked forward to seeing them alone. They were easy and familiar with Rike and affection-ate with her baby. Kehinde was both relieved that they had adjusted with apparently so little trauma, and confirmed in her opinion that there was no place for her in the family. The circle had closed in her absence, and she did not have the strength to fight her way back in.

14 Letter to Moriammo

Dear Moriammo,

I just have to write you this letter with the hope that it meets you and your family in good health. What is Olumide doing now? Playing for Manchester United? We are all right here, but there are plenty of stories, so rich and varied that if a prophet had told them to me months ago, I would have advised him to go an look for another profession.

The day I was leaving, I saw Tunde at the airport. He said he was surprised to see me. Our husbands, can't they pretend? But he didn't act well enough, and I could see the relief on his face when he realised that I was going home to be with Albert at last.

Why do our husbands feel threatened when a woman shows signs of independence by wanting to live alone for a while? Because that was the way I saw it. Remember the day you brought Olumide to 'my house'? I now call it my house, because that is exactly what it's going to be: my house, not our house. Anyway, you remember that day? How relaxed we were, like school girls. We didn't mind that the plantain we fried was half burned because we were talking. I even put on that naughty video and we watched it, just like men. I didn't see anything wrong with all that, or did you? It was harmless fun. After all, we earned more than our husbands, and we were in better jobs. So I didn't understand your reason for feeling guilty and agreeing with Tunde in shunning me. I thought our friendship had gone beyond that, and we were more like sisters. Sometimes, I even used to mistake you for my Taiwo, who left a vacuum which was only filled when I met you, nineteen years ago when we were both nervous young girls preparing to go to Britain to join our future husbands. Remember how frightened you were because you had never met Tunde before? Your parents had told you he came from a very good family, and you were carrying his photograph. Remember how we asked those horrible cooks on the ship to tell us how old the photograph was, and they said it was taken fifty years ago? We both cried, thinking that you were going to join an old man. I promised that I would look after you if you didn't like Tunde. Remember how we slept on the same bunk, clutching each other? You were very frightened because you were a virgin and you didn't know whether the first night was going to be as painful as other women had said. I assured you that it was not going to be too bad, because Albert and I had done it lots of times in his bachelor's room in Tappa Street. What a relief when we found that Tunde was as skinny as Albert. And from what you told me later, the pain on the first night was happy pain, because he was loving, and he had had a lot of experience.

It was unfortunate about the pram. We could have afforded to buy Olumide ten prams if he wanted, but just because Tunde bought it, he made so much *palava* over it. Don't tell me he didn't, I could guess from the little you told me. And after that you started behaving strangely.

Things are happening here which, as I said earlier, I would never have believed could happen. Albert – oh, I forgot, I'm not allowed to call him that-o, because I didn't give the name to him. (He didn't give me the name Kehinde, yet he is free to shout my name even in the open marketplace.) I have to say 'Joshua's father' or 'our father' or 'our husband'. He didn't come to my room until three days after my arrival, when he came in the middle of the night, and half-heartedly made as if to demand his marital rights. Of course, I refused, as I think he expected. He only came to my room to do his duty, not to be intimate or loving. He left all that in England.

My sister, Ifeyinwa, told me not to behave badly. She told

93

me to lower my voice and accept his apologies, whenever he gave them. She talked a lot of inanities, my sister. She's frightened for me. You'd like her, but looking at her, you'd think marriage was a prison. She looks about as healthy as a two-day old chick caught in the rain. And as for apologies, from Albert? He didn't make any. Why should he? After all, he did not commit a crime against humanity, all he did was marry Rike and have a baby boy, with another on the way, without my knowing anything about it. Yes, Moriammo, he has another wife. She is a lecturer. She had a PhD. She has a maid. She has a Peugeot. She has a son twelve months old. And I am sure the one she's carrying will be another son. You know my husband – our husband – cannot sit down and read a book to save his life, but now he is married to a young woman with a doctorate degree in literature!

I have been for several interviews, but as we suspected, they want younger people. When they are liberal enough to employ a woman, they want a younger one, with certificates. Unless I condescend to be a secretary, and even for that, I am not qualified. So stay with your job. Experience? No one talks of experience here. You must produce certificates or perish.

This is making my life unbearable. Albert travels a great deal. His work takes him to the north where he stays for weeks on end. When he returns, there is a kind of celebration. His sisters descend, and all the relatives present themselves, while his little wife makes *shakara* – having her bath, scenting herself, carrying on. When Albert is away, she concentrates all her energy on her university work. Honestly, Moriammo, Albert has humiliated me, and the worst is, that I have to depend on him financially. He gave me the first housekeeping money in over eighteen years of marriage, and I had to take it. When I refused to kneel to take it, his sisters levied a fine of one cock. Paying the fine took half the housekeeping. It is a man's world here. No wonder so many of them like to come home, despite their successes abroad. Honestly, if not for the children, I would have come back long ago. But now, I have no money for the fare back.

94

Can you locate Mary Elikwu for me? I tried to reach her before I left. She had been on my conscience since the night of Albert's party. She has foresight, going to college and having herself educated, after so many children. Raising children is no longer enough. The saving grace for us women is the big 'E' of education. This girl, Rike, doesn't even have to live with us because her education has made her independent, yet she is content to be an African wife in an Igbo culture. How come we in England did not see all this? I think perhaps Mary Elikwu did. Do reply soon. Your friend,

Kehinde Okolo.

When Kehinde posted this letter, she felt lighter, as if she had confessed. It was a hot day as usual, and the humidity was high for that time of day. Lagos people liked to walk slowly, dragging their feet, but this afternoon, they had more reason for doing so. Even the wind was too lazy to lift the dust from the roadside. People looked drugged with heat. Kehinde noticed a group of onlookers forming a knot on the other side of the road, but could not see what they were looking at. There was no need to hurry home so she crossed the road to see what was going on. Two men had decided to take the frustrations of life out on each other. The story was that man number one had wanted to buy a paper. He had held out twenty Naira so that the paper boy would give him change, but man number two was quicker. He snatched the twenty Naira and made a run for it, but he did not go very far. People standing around were suddenly galvanised out of their boredom and chased him. They must have been disappointed to have caught him so soon, but he had little energy for a long race. He and man number one now got into a fist fight. His story was that he had left university three months before, but could not find a job, while here was a man flashing twenty Naira for a newspaper, when he had had no food for four whole days. He asked the onlookers to judge the case. Everybody had an opinion. Some blamed the government for making young people go through the travails of western education, only to tell them at the end that there was no market for what they had struggled for. Others said that was not an excuse to steal. The older people wanted to know what man number one expected, if he flashed twenty Naira so ostentatiously in a place like Mile 2, where jobless people congregate to shelter from the noonday sun. The unanimous agreement was that they should share the twenty Naira into two. Man number two was reluctant, and was appealing to the man whose money it was to let him have it, and God would bless him for it. There was a hush as the crowd listened to this plea. The man had a sweet voice, and he spoke eloquently. Kehinde knew that he had won. All this was happening not too far away from the police station. An officer with a kwashiokor-like protruding belly sat astride a chair, his unsheathed truncheon idle at his side. He yawned and looked the other way, provoking laughter.

Kehinde shook her head and smiled. She had not travelled extensively, and the only place she could compare Lagos with was London. She could not imagine a scene like this happening there. No, this could only happen here, in Nigeria. She wiped the sweat that poured from under her *gele* and drifted away. Suddenly, the heat made her remember that this was October, autumn in England. The wind would be blowing, leaves browning and falling. In a few weeks, the cherry tree in her back garden would be naked of leaves, its dark branches twisted like old bones. On a day like this, after the Friday shopping, her feet would be stretched in front of her gas fire, while she watched her favourite serials on television until she was tired and until her eyes ached. Autumn in England.

Her eyes misted. She thought of Christmas shopping, which always used to annoy her, and longed for a brisk walk to Harrods, or Marks and Spencers, or Selfridges, just looking and buying little. She even felt nostalgia for the wet stinking body-smell of the underground.

She took hold of herself. Surely it was foolish to pine for a country where she would always be made to feel unwelcome. But then her homecoming had been nothing like the way she had dreamed of it. She now knew how naïve she had been, trusting

96

Albert implicitly. She had thought that Ifeyinwa's life could never be hers. The Africa of her dreams had been one of parties and endless celebrations, in which she, too, would enjoy the status and respect of a been-to. Instead, she found herself once more relegated to the margins.

15   Decision

Days followed nights which were hot and clammy, and in which Kehinde found it difficult to sleep, tossing on her sweat-soaked bed and waiting for morning, hoping that the new day would bring something different. It was difficult to describe her feelings, even to herself. She was waiting for something, but what that something was, she could not say.

Albert had gone north, so the house was quiet, with the exception of Grace, Rike's maid. When Rike was at the university, the rise and fall of Grace's voice would fill the house from the backyard, singing to the babies in her care, or laughing and flirting with the house boys from the other yard.

Kehinde could not summon the energy to interfere. Grace's behaviour was simply a reflection of her employers' attitude towards Kehinde, and indicated the low esteem in which she was held in the household. She was the senior wife, the been-to madam, but she did not work and she had no influence with Albert. The servants saw this, and treated her with barely concealed insolence.

Kehinde considered the day ahead, alone in the house with the servants, the only one without anything to do. She remembered Moriammo saying a long time ago, 'Just sit at home and play the white been-to madam.' She thought of the white women who came to Africa with their husbands, with nothing to do but entertain themselves, and wondered how they tolerated it. She was restless for something to happen.

'Grace . . . Grace,' she called. The laughter stopped, but there was no response. Kehinde could have fetched her own bath water, but that would have been an admission of her lack of status in the house. She had to hold onto a shred of dignity. Exerting herself, she called authoritatively: 'Grace! Grace! *abi* you deaf?'

'Yes ma, I dey come.' Grace knocked at the door, wiping her hands on her house *lappa*, in an elaborate display of having been interrupted at work.

'Good morning ma. You slept well?' Grace asked, panting as if she had been running to obey Kehinde's summons.

'Thank you. Make you carry water for my bath.'

'Yes ma, thank you ma. After bath, you wan' make I get breakfast?'

'No, thank you. But you for wash those clothes there. Make you spread am for ground under cashew tree. The sun dey fade the colours, quick, quick.'

'Yes ma.'

Fully dressed, Kehinde sauntered to the front room. There, resting on the coffee table, was a cheap envelope addressed to her. Angrily she tore it open to find it was the result of a job interview she had had three months before. The post had been filled and they wished her luck somewhere else, but did not tell her where. She was supposed to be grateful they even bothered to tell her of her failure to secure the job.

Kehinde bit her lower lip until it almost bled. She wished she had spelt out her desperation more clearly to Moriammo. She longed to return to London, but was too proud to admit it, even to herself. Nonetheless, she trusted Moriammo to read between the lines.

It was much later, as the enervating heat had at last begun to subside towards evening, that Rike knocked at her door.

'Mummy, are you resting?' she called. 'Sorry to disturb, but there is someone in the sitting-room with a message for you.'

Kehinde's heart missed a beat, but she controlled herself.

'Thank you, my daughter. How was your day?' she asked, in a voice so casual, it sounded unreal.

'It was good, thank you for asking, Mummy.'

Kehinde tied her *lappa* more securely and came out of her

room. She touched Ogochukwu on the cheek and remarked, 'Why are you holding him. Where is Grace?'

'We have run out of gas, and Grace has gone to buy a new cylinder.'

'Oh, this business of buying gas by the bottle . . .'

Rike, who had no idea how else they would buy gas, shrugged and followed Kehinde into the sitting-room. She was not going to leave her alone with the visitor. The bearer of the message was a young woman who worked as a hostess with Nigeria Airways. She and Kehinde had met once before, through Moriammo. Knowing Rike's plan, Kehinde invited the woman into her room.

The young woman followed her. She was a Nigerian brought up in a polygamous family, so there was no need to explain. She knew the necessity of hiding from the rest of the family, especially from a younger wife.

'I have a letter for you, madam,' she said conspiratorially, looking over her shoulder. Kehinde fingered the large white envelope and knew it contained more than a letter. She smiled. The young woman smiled too. 'You don't want me to give you anything to eat?'

'Thank you, but no, ma. We ought to have been in Lagos since last night, but you know how it is with our planes.'

Kehinde nodded. 'I know how it is with us. But no matter. This is Nigeria . . .'

Laughingly, they chorused, 'Please bear with us.'

Kehinde tore the letter open as soon as the girl had left. Moriammo had sent her the fare. She quickly skimmed the letter, which referred only briefly to the money. 'This is a long loan, payable when able. Don't forget that we both worked in a bank for over ten years, and interest always goes with loans! But also, don't let fear of what people will say stop you from doing what your *chi* wants.

The house is still there and so are your tenants, though the house is going downhill. The kitchen ceiling collapsed after a recent storm, but your Caribbean man promised to repair it. The last time I saw him at the shopping centre, he asked of you. I think he likes you, now that you are far away. Our men are the same – they value what is beyond their reach. I am beginning to like him too, now that I know him better.

The honeymoon with Tunde over the birth of his heir, Olumide, is long over. I have secured him his immortality, so I don't need to be humoured any more. Also, Olumide is beginning to cost us a packet in nursery fees. But you know me, live and let live. I am not moaning or anything like that. In fact, I worry for Tunde, how someone can be so stingy, even to himself. He won't miss a day's work so as not to lose that stupid commission they give him at Nigeria Airways.

It's lucky that Alby decided to go polygamous in Nigeria and not here in London. It would have been much worse for you here. Please come back as soon as you want to. By the way, the interest I mentioned earlier is a joke, just in case Nigeria has made you lose your sense of humour. You keep the money. It's a way of saying I am sorry for being such a wet blanket.

That your Mrs Elikwu is in the news lately. She has just published a children's book of myths and legends, and she is a spokesperson for the 'Milk for our babies' campaign. I don't think you need have her on your conscience. She must know by now, what we women are like. When we are married, we feel we have an advantage over a woman who is living by herself, even if the latter is a million times happier. I'm sure she'll understand. God bless you, my sister, and write soon.'

Kehinde read the letter again and again, and each time she smiled at the end of it. Moriammo must have copied the letter many times, as Kehinde had never met anyone with Moriammo's education who was so lazy about writing English. Moriammo said she had never met a language with so many rules that could be broken. In the case of this letter, she must have spent hours getting it right. Kehinde felt deeply gratified by Moriammo's gestures of friendship. For the first time, a way out of her situation had presented itself. She looked at her watch. There was still time to go to Ikorodu Grammar and see Bimpe and Joshua.

Outside the house, she looked back, and saw Rike peeping

from behind the net curtains. Kehinde smiled. It reminded her of her London neighbours.

The school caretaker met her reluctantly, protesting that five o'clock was not the visiting hour and the students were busy doing their homework. Kehinde's plea that it was urgent failed to move him, but a folded note discreetly slipped into his palm, as she had seen Albert do at the airport, transformed him in an instant. He bowed several times, thanking her repeatedly, before he disappeared to fetch the children.

Less than five minutes later, Joshua and Bimpe rushed expectantly into the reception area.

'Heh, special mum, what's the matter?' Bimpe cried.

As they embraced, she assured them that everything was fine and asked about their health and their studies. They in turn told her they were getting on well. Then there was a short silence. The children knew Kehinde had not come there on a non-visiting day just to inquire about their health. Kehinde said suddenly, 'Look, I don't want to keep you from your work, but I want you to know that I am going back to London.'

The children stared at her and Bimpe's face fell.

'You quarrelled with Dad?' she wanted to know.

'No, no, nothing like that. He is still in the north. I just want to go back, get a job, and look after the house. Aunty Moriammo says it is falling apart . . .'

'Shouldn't Dad be doing that?' Joshua asked.

'He has a good job here and a new family . . .' Kehinde tentatively explained. Bimpe burst into tears.

'But you're the backbone of the family, Ma. Why do you want to run away?'

'Bimpe, you can come any time you like, you know that,' Kehinde hastened to reassure her.

'What of Dad, can he come too, or are you going to divorce him because of Rike?'

Kehinde was taken aback by Bimpe's insight, but all she said was, 'No, Bimpe, it's not quite like that. I have to go for my own sanity. Moriammo has sent me the money for the fare, and I'll be leaving soon. I want you to take care of each other, and I'll

102

write to you.' Kehinde could see the caretaker hovering by the door, so she embraced them quickly and slipped away.

It was not so easy to slip away from Ifeyinwa.

'I knew it! I felt it!' Ifeyinwa cried. 'To London, to do what? England your country now, *abi*?'

'No, England no be my country, but I wan go back *sha*. See me here, I no get job, I no get nothing. Just siddon for home, dey wait for Albert. And when he return self, na im junior wife he wan see, not be me. I wan go back.'

'But you know our parents' tory. For years our Mama dey carry palm-kernel to market for Asaba. When she don sell finish, she use the money pay our Papa school fees. When Papa done school finish, he return for Lagos come get job for railway. By that time, Mama no look fresh any more for Papa to introduce to his friends. Then Papa marry that other one. Mama don dey think say she go make our Papa love her if she born more pikin. But our Papa just shun her. But she self she no fit think of leaving us her children and running away!

And I tell you one thing else. Na you be the trouble that finish her. Na you wey eat up your sister for Mama belle.'

'Oh, for God's sake, Ifeyinwa. You did Biology at school. How could I have eaten my sister? And why is my birth the first thing everyone refers to whenever I try to do something for myself?'

'I know you hurt because Albert don marry another wife. Over there for London, no be one man, one wife? But our way different. How come the day you marry, our parents say to you, "Make you look after this man, like your child, so he can help you raise your children"? Na so it be. You no feel for nobody. What of your children?'

'Joshua and Bimpe? *Sebi*, you are here? Albert's sisters and even Rike all love them. They are enjoying the attention. I have spoken to them already, so they know. When I get there, I'll see if I can get qualified for something, and bring them over.'

'Then make you get belle before you go, so you go get another child.'

Tears came to Kehinde's eyes. She said in a strangled voice, 'I don't want any more children. I have tied my tubes.'

Ifeyinwa opened her eyes wide and swallowed hard. Then she crossed herself. The shock of what Kehinde had said left her speechless. For once in her life, Ifeyinwa could find no words with which to answer her sister.

Worst thing that could happen

16   Return to London

Ifeyinwa was sobbing as if her heart would break. 'How will I ever hold up my head again? Now, everybody will say to Albert, "Did we not warn you about her? Did we not warn you about her family? They are no good." Look around you Kehinde, do you see any of our brothers or their wives come to see you off? They are not here because you've shamed us all. They pretend not to know you are leaving today. I sent my son Amechi to tell them all . . .' Ifeyinwa's sobs were almost uncontrollable.

'Little mother, Ifi, we've been through all this several times before. I was a fool not to have seen this side of Albert before, but now that I've seen it, I can't take it.'

'Just listen to you, as if we are savages . . .'

'No, Ifeyinwa, you know I don't mean that. I had never lived in a polygamous family before, except when I came to visit you, and I was already estranged from you before I left Nigeria. I knew only Aunty Nnebogo and then the convent. Albert was raised in a polygamous family and so were you. I don't want us to go through all this again now. Joshua and Bimpe understand. Try to look at things through my eyes. I promise to help you financially whenever I can. Being without Albert in London means I will be free to decide what to do with my money.'

'Father should not have allowed them to take you away. They should have told you the story of your birth right from the start. They should have raised you with the rest of us.'

Kehinde felt tired. She suddenly longed to get away to the peace of her own home. As soon as her luggage had been checked in, she said good-bye to Ifeyinwa and headed for the departure lounge, to avoid any more tears. No sooner had she settled herself on the dark-grey metal bench to wait for her flight, than a tap on her shoulder made her turn her head. 'Oh, Ifeyinwa, how did you manage to wrangle you way in here?' she exclaimed. 'This is meant for passengers only.'

'We still dey for Nigeria, *abi* you don forget? A small dash goes a long way here.' She sighed. 'I wish I could go with you.'

'Eh, what's happening here? Outside that partition you were reminding me of my duty and responsibility. Now you wan' come with me?'

'I know what I said. But you are a twin, and you must do what your *chi* tells you. Twins are difficult to predict.'

'Is that what you slipped through the partition to tell me?'

Ifeyinwa nodded. Then she added as an afterthought, 'I've heard that Albert's got a sweetheart in the north. I think Rike suspects.'

There was a long silence before Kehinde responded. 'Poor Albert, how will he cope with all his responsibilities?' She picked up one of Ifeyinwa's hands and held it in both of hers. 'Thank you for telling me, but why did you try to persuade me to stay if you knew this?'

Ifeyinwa shrugged her thin shoulders. 'At least no one can go about blaming me for not trying to keep you here. In terms of tradition, I have done my sisterly duty. Now let us talk down-to-earth.' Ifeyinwa asked in a voice harsh with rebellion, 'Tell me, little sister, when you get there, are you going to take another man?'

Kehinde feigned shock. 'After you've told me that the man who took me to the altar is about to take a third wife?' A mischievous grin lit Ifeyinwa's pinched face. For the first time, Kehinde glimpsed the spirit trapped behind the veneer of tradition.

'Go on, will you?' she persisted.

'You told me the other day that I was still young. I'm not going to sew myself up with a needle, or lock myself up with a padlock. From what I can gather, that particular freedom is one of the joys of polygamy.'

'And Albert's other wife?' Ifeyinwa asked, now smiling broadly. Again, Kehinde regretted not having had the opportunity to get to know her sister properly.

'Well, Rike will be responsible for the well-being of Joshua and Bimpe during the holidays.'

'You're learning fast. I'll have a few surprises of my own for her after you've gone.'

'What surprises?'

'Ah, you keep your secrets and I'll keep mine. But rest assured, Albert is not going to gain a Naira from that house in England.'

Kehinde wished she could take her sister with her. She could see that Ifeyinwa was going to miss her. She was now a grandmother and was expected to behave like one, but she could pass for thirty-five, and the body she had used all these years in nurturing and caring still yearned for comfort. Kehinde hugged her and whispered, 'Now sis, no more tears. I will send for you when I can afford it, at least for a short visit.' Ifeyinwa hugged her back. 'I know you will, and I shall certainly come. So see you in London.'

At Heathrow, to Kehinde's surprise, even the immigration officers were welcoming. Generally, anyone coming from Nigeria was routinely sniffed for drugs by specially trained dogs, and subjected to all sorts of questioning at the immigration counter, but Kehinde was waved through.

Outside, though it was cold, the sun was shining, and she felt a surge of elation. She got out of the taxi in front of the house in Leyton, and was surprised that nothing had changed in the twelve months she had been away. She did not know what changes she had been expecting but it looked as if things had stood still. Only a few hours before, still in Nigeria, she had thought the whole world was collapsing. Now she noticed that the trees the council had planted along the street were just beginning to bud. In a few days, they would burst into bloom, and it would be spring.

Kehinde dipped her hand into her coat pocket and brought out the front door key. When it fitted, she was surprised.

Inside the narrow hallway, the smell of the London terrace

107

house welcomed her like a lost child. Before she could suppress it, a voice inside her sang out, 'Home, sweet home!' Taiwo, who had not spoken to her since she had gone to Nigeria, was back. Kehinde rebuked the voice: 'This is not my home. Nigeria is my home.' As she said it, she knew she was deceiving herself, and Taiwo would not let her get away with it. 'We make our own choices as we go along,' came the voice. 'This is yours. There's nothing to be ashamed of in that.'

'Yes, but,' Kehinde found herself arguing, 'this is a country where people think if you talk to your *chi* that you're talking to yourself, and if you talk to yourself, you must be mad.' A cold draught blew round her ankles, and she realised she had not yet closed the door. The For Sale sign flapped forlornly in the wind. Something propelled her back outside, and with unexpected strength she wrenched it from the ground. 'This house is not for sale,' she declared. 'This house is mine.'

17 Ifeyinwa

Whenever Ifeyinwa saw people off at the airport, which merci-
fully was not often, her grief was not just for the departure, but
arose from an irrepressible fear of permanent loss. She was,
therefore, all the more relieved to hear from Kehinde of her safe
arrival. From lively, noisy, colourful Lagos, Ifeyinwa could only
picture Kehinde in London as cold and lonely. She felt deep
regret that she had not stayed, especially as she had appeared to
want to when she arrived. Had she not brought most of the
furniture from their London house back to Lagos? Had she not
resigned her job? Ifeyinwa had hoped that now, at last, she
would be able to enjoy her sister, but she had been thwarted. In
a life of deprivation, she felt passionately that this was one
privilege to which she should have been entitled.

Nor was it just the emotional bond which meant so much to
her. Ifeyinwa and her children lived at a level of poverty that
even Kehinde's small contributions, filched from Albert's housekeeping, alleviated. For days, she walked around frozen, sucking
her teeth whenever anyone crossed her path. Her brain, however,
was extremely active, working out how she could best take
revenge on Albert and Rike, to whom she attributed responsibility for driving Kehinde away.

Ifeyinwa, for years accustomed to accepting what life threw at
her, baulked at the loss of her sister for the third time. As a child,
she had pined for her dead mother's only other girl-child.
Growing up among brothers, at the mercy of her step-mother,
she had woven a fantasy around her missing sister every bit as
poignantly felt as Kehinde's for her Taiwo. As a young wife, she

109

had stolen away from her domestic duties, leaving her children with the maid, to visit Kehinde in school, taking her small gifts she could not afford. Even Kehinde's obvious distaste for her family set-up and the increasing reserve she maintained, did not deter her.

When Kehinde left for England to marry Albert, Ifeyinwa felt it as a bereavement. For twenty-odd years she had mourned her sister's absence, punctuated only by Christmas cards with the briefest of messages, occasional snapshots of the children, and once, just once, a twenty pound note, which she had used to buy school books for her children. Then the news had come, Albert was returning. Next came Joshua and Bimpe, whom she had never seen. Ifeyinwa was ready to take them to her heart as her own children, but Rike intervened. She had watched her insinuate herself into Albert's household, playing on his loneliness, soothing his vanity, helping out with his motherless children. She had watched, and said nothing, as Rike's belly grew and Albert fell prey to the alluring visions of the prophets and married her. When Kehinde announced her own arrival, Ifeyinwa made certain she was there, to welcome and warn and comfort her. Her allegiance never faltered, no matter how much Albert's sisters attempted to humiliate her, or Rike smirked. As long as she had Kehinde there in Lagos, Ifeyinwa felt she had some compensation for her own joyless life, someone to whom she could talk freely without fear of exposure. Now she was gone, and vengeance was the only thing left. If she could not bring her sister back, she would make Rike's stay in Albert's house like sitting bare bottom on a chair smeared with red hot pepper, like having a piece of bone lodged in the throat, unable to swallow or to spit it out. She would ugly her life. Was Kehinde not the only sister she had?

In the intense heat of the afternoon, Ifeyinwa left one of her children, Nwalor, to mind her stall of oranges and bananas. Nwalor could peel oranges without cutting into the flesh or cutting her fingers. She dressed for visiting and left the house.

Her reception from Rike was warm and welcoming, and so loud it could almost have been sincere. She gave Ifeyinwa a large glass of expensive imported juice, which Ifeyinwa accepted gratefully, smacking her lips to show her appreciation. All the while she watched Rike, the contented wife of a been-to man, and her resolve never wavered.

'I've heard from your mate . . . your Mummy,' Ifeyinwa began, using the endearment Lagos women used towards each other.

'Eh, so she arrived there safely!' responded Rike, innocently. 'Thanks be to the Almighty. I prayed and fasted for her to reach with no mishap.'

Beneath her calm demeanour, something terrible was boiling inside Ifeyinwa. She wanted to say, 'You mean, you gave thanks for her departure,' but resisted. She did not want to be called a witch for voicing her spite. Instead, she spoke as innocently as Rike: 'Indeed, your prayers must have worked wonders! My sister had no problems on her journey, even at their immigration check point, where they say the white officers pounce on Nigerian women and ask them to undo their hair. God listened to your prayers, thank you, my daughter.' Before Rike was able to respond in kind, Ifeyinwa asked casually, 'But you did not come to the airport?'

'Aunty Ifi, my Mummy did not tell me. I learned of her departure from Grace, you know, my house-girl. And of course the neighbours confirmed her story. She did not even tell our husband. Mummy must have been very angry to take such a drastic step.' Rike's head was bent to one side, a picture of theatrical sorrow. Had Ifeyinwa's mission not been so important, she would have burst out laughing. She had seen such scenes played out many times in her own household, where she was an old hand at the game of sharing her husband with another woman. Compared to her, Rike was a novice.

She sighed deeply and looked around the tastefully furnished living-room, noting a piece of decorative mat here and a beautiful glass vase there, brought from England by her sister to decorate her home. Her eyes came to rest on the woman in front of her, a delicate young woman with her feet in a pair of dainty white sandals. She looked away, to hide her burning hatred and anger.

She was too experienced to lay all the blame on Rike, when Rike was only operating in comformity with the system which pepetrated this kind of injustice. One woman worked hard to buy all these things and ship them across the ocean for the enjoyment of her family, and at the end of it, what happened? Another, opportunist, '*oyokoyo*' woman, who had had no part in the dream, who did not know the trouble she had taken, was now enjoying it all. To Ifeyinwa, Rike was a whited sepulchre, and Albert was Judas Iscariot. She remembered her mother's life story and swore inwardly that it would not be repeated in Kehinde.

Ifeyinwa's feelings were so intense, she had to lower her eyes to prevent Rike from reading her expression. Though Rike was younger, Ifeyinwa did not underestimate her powers. The sect she belonged to, the Cherubim and Seraphim, watched and studied others as a form of ritual. They spent so much time praying for their sins, and concentrating on their enemies, real or imagined, that Ifeyinwa knew for certain that Rike was not taken in by her expressions of good will. She knew perfectly well that Ifeyinwa had no reason to love her, and was simply pretending to be oblivious. It was a struggle for dominance, in which Rike's weapon was her assumption of innocence. But Ifeyinwa, too, could prevaricate. Right now, she was playing a simple-minded, older woman. She had worn a mask for eighteen years and nobody but Kehinde had seen behind it. If only Kehinde had stayed, together they would have ousted this interloper. Rike was a fledgling, with all her spurious religious backing. But Kehinde's *chi* had made her give up, and Ifeyinwa was left to fight alone. She sat up now and looked at Rike directly, gathering herself for the attack.

Ifeyinwa had spent long enough in school to speak the Queen's English when the occasion demanded. She drawled, 'Never mind, daughter, your Mummy did the right thing. I know my sister. She could have put up with you as a second wife, but to learn that a third is on the way, and that third is one quite uneducated and a Muslim . . . well her only qualification is that she is very beautiful. You know, the northern Fulani type of beauty, which we short-legged southerners can never compete with. For my

112

sister, that was the last straw. She wasn't going to lower herself to the level of sharing her husband with a child like that – sixteen or so. Hm! Our men, they poke any hole. Pity you couldn't cut off Albert's thing and keep it in the south, whenever he travels.' She laughed mirthlessly at her own crude joke.

Ifeyinwa stopped to catch her breath and to watch the effect of her words on the listener. The secure big-madam smile that had been playing on Rike's lips had disappeared, and her lips had become thin and stretched. Her eyes had grown larger as her body shrank deeper into Kehinde's chair. But Ifeyinwa had not quite finished. 'Anyway,' she ran on, mercilessly, 'Albert can always run back to London, whenever he gets bored here. You know our men.'

'Who will run to London? You mean, Our Father? Well, he won't find the time. What of his job? And the fares to London are going up and up.' Rike, like a corpse temporarily infused with life, spoke in a strange, harsh voice. Ifeyinwa was taken aback, seeing for the first time what Rike would look like in a few years time. One good thing about youth and beauty is that they do not last very long. In no time at all, the young woman sitting before her would no doubt be as thin, disappointed and hurt as she was.

'Naira is falling in the world market. Trips to London are soon going to be only for the very rich.' Rike was clutching at straws, her brow concertinaed like that of an old woman.

'Albert is not poor, surely. He has a house in London, remember? Not just a house, a home really. All these things you see around you are from there. It took my sister and Albert over sixteen years to build that home!' Ifeyinwa was talking with her whole body, holding her waist as if to squeeze more horrible words from inside her. Squaring her thin shoulders, she exclaimed, 'Really, so Naira is falling down! Hm, hei, terrible for Nigeria. But as for Albert, mark my words, he will still go and meet his sweetheart. When they cause enough *wahala* in one place, they move to another. It's easy for them, they don't drag children with them. Our men!'

Ifeyinwa rose majestically. She gave Rike one long animal

stare, like a predator assessing its victim. Rike was transfixed by its naked malignancy. When Ifeyinwa spoke, it was with her usual vagueness. 'I don't want to delay you. I must go now. I left Nwalor to mind the stall.' She was out of the house before Rike could move or speak. Her eyes shone with triumph as she hurried home, saying to herself: 'God forgive me, but people – man or woman – should not reap where they did not sow. I leave the other one to you, Lord.'

Ifeyinwa did not do what she had done lightly. It was a last resort, the duty of a big sister, once the mother was dead. She had done enough work for one afternoon, enough to keep Rike's mother and her *wolis* busy for a while. The *wolis* would eat at Rike's expense for a few days, their prayer, 'Give us this day, our daily bread,' answered.

Nwalor had decided that selling an orange for ten kobo was too slow, so she had been selling them for less. Ifeyinwa had made a loss, but for once it did not matter. She had gained something sweeter than money – the satisfaction of exerting her power in her sister's interests. She smiled at Nwalor, who – having expected a scolding – ran away happily to play with her friends.

18 The Woli's Vision

Rike woke from her trance to find her life in ruins. She called absentmindedly to Grace to give her a head-tie, and prepared to go to the praying-ground. It was an instinctive reaction, and she drove there without thinking. Everything she saw was unfocused – the sticks of sugarcane, the orange-sellers by the gutter on the left side of the road. It was nearing evening, and the heat of the sun was less intense.

The car left the tarred road and crunched into a pebbly footpath, leading to a huge open space surounding a tiny white-walled church building with a dusty galvanised roof. The open space was partly enclosed by white-painted walls. Worshippers often preferred to pray outside, under the umbrella trees and hibiscus bushes. The open space was almost like the interior of a church itself.

Rike had not been aware how fast she had driven, as though pursued by demons. She could see clearly Kehinde and Albert making love, Albert never returning to her. Her anxious and over-active imagination conjured up images of innumerable relatives and friends who had left for England and America, promising to be back in a couple of years. Two decades later, despite complaints about racism, unemployment, dignity robbed, they would still be there. If Albert should go again, Rike knew he would fall into the same trap. If he gave up his job just to go and sell his house, well, jobs for the uncertificated were becoming few and far between in Nigeria. Here, job applicants had to be young, loaded with certificates and not necessarily experienced.

A knot of praying people and a few *wolis* looked up at the roar of the car. Luckily her mother, Mama Abeni, was there, sitting on a low stool under the biggest and oldest umbrella tree, favoured by the *wolis* because it gave the most shade. She got up from her stool, her hands outstretched as though in benediction. One or two *wolis* who were padding barefoot from one hut to the other looked up and continued their slow walk. Rike was not the type to drive up to this holy place raising so much dust for nothing. Something must be wrong. They did not appear interested, however, but watched with the corners of their eyes, wondering at the reason for her agitation. As Rike got out of the car, her mother moved closer, hands still raised, and the other worshippers stood back.

'Mind how you walk, daughter,' Mama Abeni greeted in a controlled voice.

'Thank God for a lovely evening, Mothers and Fathers.' Rike acknowledged all present in her greeting.

'The baby, Ogochukwu, is he all right?'

'And his second?'

'Your husband?'

'Nothing wrong with him?'

'His job, going on well?'

'Your job, going on well?'

'The one with no name you're carrying, kicking well?'

As Rike nodded in answer to all these questions, with her mother intoning, 'Lord be praised' at each nod, her hither-to crushing load became lighter. Through their greetings, the worshippers were pointing out worse calamities. After the last question, she even found it difficult to start talking about her worries. The women noted her hesitation and burst out singing, 'Count your blessings, name them one by one.' By the end of the song, a circle of people holding hands surrounded her. Rike confessed that the heavy load she had been carrying seemed to have evaporated, but she began to tell them nonetheless.

'A woman came to me a short while ago. Not just an ordinary woman, my mate's sister. She came purposely to make me unhappy. She told many lies, but behind the lies were some of my fears. She said my husband would leave me and go back to

116

my mate, his first wife, in England. That my husband is intending to marry another woman, this time from the north. He meets many beautiful girls on his travels. I am afraid . . .' Once she had started, Rike poured out her soul. Where would she go with three children? How could she pay for the big house they rented and maintain a house-girl? Soon the children would be needing money to pay their school fees. Her voice rose and fell, and they allowed her to talk herself out. Time was nothing. Each person fixed their eyes on the ground, and she talked with confidence. The *wolis* were sworn to secrecy, and Rike knew she could trust them. She was one of their favourite daughters. This particular Christian community had prayed for and comforted her through school. When she had invited Albert, whom she had met by sheer accident, to their Harvest Thanksgiving a few years ago, the community immediately knew her desires, by watching and noting the way she stole glances at him. It was easy to encourage her to talk about him. When they learned he had a wife abroad and was looking for a job, they invited him for a special prayer session, during which they saw a vision for him. They said he would get a special job that God had kept for him. They said he would marry a new wife, and the child borne by this new wife would be his saviour. It was easy for Albert, a been-to with a shiny Jaguar and Rike, a successful graduate, to slide into serious friendship. The relationship represented the kind of freedom Albert had longed for in England, but could not get. Rike was a typical Lagos girlfriend, who did not ask any questions. She was happy to have a man approved by her church, and not just an ordinary man, but a polished one who spoke with a sophistication that at first used to take her breath away. She had never been attracted to those loud-mouthed Lagos boasters. Albert was cool, and very dark with teeth that shone, and he knew how to dress. After their night-long celebration on his getting a new job, she told him a few weeks later that she was pregnant. They had a traditional wedding which was blessed by Rike's church. Albert's sisters, Mama Kaduna and Aunt Mary were overjoyed, and when Rike gave birth to baby Ogochukwu, Albert became a convert to the church. He began to enjoy a life-style he could only have dreamt of in England. They had two cars, two servants, lovely weather and an easy and active social life. Rike went to the praying place several times a week and hung on every word that came out of the mouths of the *wolis*. Albert was busy travelling, but he felt Rike and her mother, Mama Abeni, were praying enough for the two of them.

Then Kehinde had decided to return. The *wolis* told Rike not to worry, that such women were always too arrogant to share their husbands and would soon leave. When Rike realised that Kehinde was indeed leaving, Mama Abeni and her women friends fasted for days until her departure. They did this without the knowledge of the male *wolis*.

By the time Rike had reached the end of her story, the *wolis* encircling her were like a barricade against evil. There were seven of them, to symbolise the seven days of God's creation. They hailed God in seven different languages at the same time, calling God His seven different names. They begged him to come down and listen to the plea of His handmaiden, Rike. Sweat poured from their faces, and the robes that had before hung loosely were now wet and clinging to their bodies. Rike cried until she was tired of crying, but the *wolis* went on wailing to God. Rike's knees started to hurt from kneeling on the sand, so she decided to sit down, especially as she was several months pregnant. The women suddenly started to leap, and after seven leaps, one of them shouted, 'They . . . they . . . should tell . . . tell . . . that man – Albert – that . . . that . . . if he ever sets foot in England again . . . again . . . he will die the death.' Everybody gasped. Rike fell to her knees again. She did not want Albert to die. The prophetess continued, 'The calamity would come from his first woman. The woman, Albert's first wife had two spirits working in her. We don't know if she was one of a twin or not, but there are two forces inside her. She is destined to live very long, having two lives in one. Such people are like fire. Anybody who crosses their path is licked out of existence.' Finally, the warning came: Rike and Albert should beware and not interfere with her hold on the house in England. A loud and haunted wail followed this announcement. A male *woli* took up the refrain as the others groaned.

'Did we not foretell that Albert would get a job? Did we not tell him that he would get a new wife and then a child who would one day bring him good luck in all his undertakings? If he should leave the Christian life God has thus prepared for him, he would lose the glory. God would turn His back on him, and he would not see His face. That woman is evil. When she was a child they took her to an evil place to placate her second spirit, and now the two of them work together, hand-in-hand, in this world. Albert needs our prayers, and a long fast, otherwise I foresee calamities. You have to call him, quick, quick. The calamity is just around the corner. Tell him to come here . . .'

'He is still away on tour, Father. He will be back in a week or two. He is still in the north,' said Rike tremulously.

Mama Abeni, her mother, stretched out a hand and helped her daughter up. 'We will keep our minds on him, so he will return safely. But as soon as he returns, tell him to come here. He needs our prayers.'

'Go on being a good and obedient wife, my daughter, the kind of wife Sarah was to Abraham, quiet, full of good works, and God-fearing. God will reward you and the fruit of your womb,' concluded the eldest *woli*.

The male *wolis'* 'amens' were short and crisp, then they walked briskly back into the church. The women sat around Rike, exhausted and empty. In a low voice, Rike's mother told her she should bring a white goat, without spot, twelve cans of milk, seven loaves of bread and a basket of assorted fruits.

'The *wolis* are going into a period of fasting for you. They will need the food after the fast,' explained a young female *woli* sitting on the ground. She was making drawings on the sand, as if calculating what it was going to cost. Rike was not at all concerned at the expense, so grateful was she for the lessening of her burden.

19   Starting Again

Dear Special Mother,

I hope you are well. We are trying to live and like it here, and we are all physically okay.

You know, don't you, Mother, that Dad has lost his job? It happened suddenly. One minute, he had a job, the next he was sacked. I knew then that I would have to be a day girl. Dad did not ask me to leave the dormitory, but I knew it would be much cheaper for him. He thanked me very much for making the gesture. Rike drives me to school most mornings, because our school is not too far from the university.

Joshua is staying in the boarding house. He did not volunteer to be a day student and nobody is expecting him to do so. You know, mum, how much is expected of boys here. He works so hard at his studies, you just can't believe it's the same Joshua. He's working for his 'O' Levels and if he goes through, he will have to take his pre-university JAMB examination. I still don't understand the system very well. So many exams to take. People are neurotic about certificates here. I suppose it's because if you don't have a good education, you perish. I would like to pass my exams but I don't particularly like school here anymore. It's always study, study, study. Young people don't live here, they just work, and when I return from school, the amount of house work I am expected to do, Ma, it's incredible. My friends say I feel this way because I was born in England and can easily go back to London. Maybe they're right. But Nigeria is great too. I like the clothes, the weather, the music, but you need a lot of money to enjoy all this. If your Dad is not working and the only income coming in is from his second wife, then life is no joke. Most of my friends still think that England is the gateway to Heaven, and I think they are right sometimes.

Why can't they provide more paying jobs here so that people like Dad who don't particularly like it in Europe can stay? Because here is nice also. Daddy's health is bad. I worry about him all the time. I think the cause of his ill health is because he's unhappy about being jobless. He's written so many applications, and been promised so many jobs, but none have materialised. And all these promises cost a lot of money. Daddy has to tip everybody connected with the job, from the management to the top executive, only that here they call it 'oiling the palms' or crudely speaking, just old fashioned bribe.

Now Dad has given up looking for work. He just sits around reading old newspapers. I don't know what he is searching for. Mum, I must tell you about Dad's wife, Rike. She is not bad, you know. I think she loves Daddy. She takes him to her church. They really do great dancing in that church. They came to the house the other day and said special prayers for Dad to get a job. They said he would get a new job when God forgave him. I wish God would forgive him soon, because I suspect that Rike's income is not nearly enough. I have heard them arguing about money when they didn't know I was listening.

Mum, when are you going to send for Joshua and me? Please don't abandon us here. I know it was painful for you, what Dad did. Joshua and I were shocked at first, but we soon learnt that it is very common here. And Rike is not bad at all. She prays for all of us all the time. And we are family, Mum.

I suggested to Dad to come and stay there in London with you for a while, but he didn't want to discuss it. Are you going to be nasty to him if he comes? Why don't you write and invite him, at least to see a doctor? You used to be such good friends, you and Dad. Mum, please don't be too hard. I love all the members of my family. I have many mothers, but you will

121

always come first, not just because you carried me for nine months before I was born, but because you are a special person.

Food is becoming more and more expensive. It would be nice if you could help us out, at least Joshua and me, so we too could help others. Your sister, Aunty Ifeyinwa, cooks good food and invites Joshua and me to eat in her house. She won't let us bring Ogochukwu with us. She's not sorry for Dad at all, she says he deserves what he gets. How can any person deserve not to get a job? She is nice, but I don't like it when she talks that way. But we can't afford to do without her food.

Do you still see Aunty Moriammo? Give her my love. One day, I will thank her specially for sending you the fare. You would not have been able to afford to go otherwise. Her son Olumide must be big now. I can't wait to see him.

Oh, I almost forgot – congratulations! I can't believe that in such a short time, a little over three years, you could get a degree! I know you said you were determined to be a university graduate, but honestly Mum, I didn't think you could achieve it. Many congratulations, Mum.

And thank you for the pocket money you sent us through the air hostess. I have given Aunty Ifeyinwa her share. Mama Kaduna and Aunt Mary send their regards.

I give you a thousand kisses.

Goodbye Special Mum and take care,

Bimpe

'Why is thy countenance sad?' Duro asked. They were in a small dark service room of the hotel where they worked, La Duchess.

'It's sad because I'm confused. I had a letter from Bimpe this morning.' Duro's face beamed, and she took the marking pencil from her mouth. 'Eh, God's child!' she cried, 'Bimpe, with the deep feelings. Did she say that they are all well?'

'Yes, she said everybody's okay.'

'No rumble-belly, no headache, no rheumatism?'

Kehinde laughed. 'You never take life seriously, do you Duro?'

'Nope. The day I go die, I wan party for seven days non stop, with plenty, plenty music, for day and night.'

'Not in this cold London, you won't. Duro, I beg, shut the door.'

The room became closer still, but by shutting the door, they avoided the guests who had a way of surprising them. The hotel passage had muted lights and a deep grey carpet, a complete contrast to the tiny room in which they worked. Huge carpet sweepers leaned heavily against piles of linen, toilet rolls and bales of towels, which blocked the tiny windows. In summer, their side of the building caught the sun directly, and they sweltered.

'She wants to come back to London. Not just herself, but Joshua too.'

'So, that surprises you? *Sebi* they can read? Even the children can see the writing on the wall. The military government is messing up again. Festac carnival is now over. *Yamutu*! Everybody is running back to London to do *gburu*. It's always "monkey dey work, baboon dey chop." When we don do all the work, we go give it back to the west again in loan repayments. And then we sit back and blame them.'

'But this new military government promised to improve on the old one after the coup. I don't understand why we keep inviting tief to come, time and time again. Now our children no even wan stay there.'

'Hmm . . . Kehinde, don't you know that if the money is right, we will sell ourselves to the devil? I don't waste time deceiving myself, I'm beginning to give up hope for our country. If the place is well run, will we be here working as hotel room cleaners? You with all your sociology degree and me with my so many diplomas?'

'Yes,' Kehinde agreed, 'you see all those women cleaning the underground, they are qualified as we are, but they do it because the pay is enough to live on. In Nigeria, with the exception of the corrupt politicians, very few honest people can make a living

123

from their profession. All that is not doing anything for our dignity, I know, but that is how it is. The children want to earn good money. Life here will be easier for them than it has been for us. After all, they were born here. But I thought they would have stayed a little longer.'

'Stayed a little longer, doing what?' Duro asked, laughing. 'You could not take the daily stress in Lagos yourself. I think you wandered too far into the market, like the child in the fable. We are condemned to spend the best part of our lives serving the so-called Mother Country, pouring fresh African blood into her tired veins to keep her going. It's nice to keep thinking we can get out and go back one day and live happily ever after, but I've seen better qualified people killing themselves to come here and do even these menial jobs we are complaining about. You want your children to be really free? Well, they are free to make this choice. Many of their mates at home would love to have such opportunity.'

'Duro, is that really the way you see it?'

'Is there any other way? Maybe in the future things may change. Maybe there'll be fewer corrupt leaders in our part of the world, but until then, our best brains will always run away to work for the white man.'

Kehinde sighed. 'If only I fit get better job to save for their fares.'

'Why don't you take the evening job going on this floor as well, just for a month or two?'

They stopped talking. Their ears had been trained to listen for quiet steps on the thick carpet, and they knew them quite well. It was their supervisor, Mr Butterworth, approaching. Kehinde started to count the folded sheets frantically, making much noise about it. Chubby Mr Butterworth opened the door, unannounced.

'Number twenty-eight is checking out, and the new guests are at the airport. Kehinde, you'd better go and do the suite first. He's an Arab. I think he's bringing his family as well.'

'Excuse me, sir,' broke in Kehinde, 'I would like to do a few extra hours in the evenings.'

124

'You mean the day shift's not enough for you? I really don't know where you girls get all your energy from. Don't you have any social life at all?' Nobody answered him. He twisted his head to ease the hotel tie, which was apparently making him uncomfortable. He looked closely at the two black faces staring at him, and shrugged. 'Mind you,' he added, 'the evening shift is lighter, because there are usually no beds to be made. Yes, you can look after this floor in the evenings.'

'Oh, thank you, thank you very much. This,' continued Kehinde, windmilling her arms like her sister Ifeyinwa, 'is our social life.'

'You mean money is at the root of it?'

'Oh Mr Butterworth, tell us what evil doesn't have money at its root?' joked Duro.

'Ah, this is not for evil purposes-o, my friend,' declared Kehinde. 'The money I get here is life itself to me and my family.'

Duro laughed, displaying her white teeth. 'As for me, when I started, my pay was the icing on the cake, now it's the cake, or rather, bread.'

Mr Butterworth viewed them both with embarrassment, but at least he had agreed to the extra work. He padded out, leaving Kehinde to prepare the suite for the sheik and his family.

'See, jobs are easy to get here,' Duro commented.

'I wrote seventy-two applications to banks, begging to be considered for the kind of job I was doing before I left for Nigeria. That was before I got a degree, too,' lamented Kehinde.

'You got that job a long time ago, and you were stupid to leave. You can't get such jobs now. You never know, with your degree you may even be regarded as being over-qualified. An educated black person in a responsible job is too much of a threat. White people don't feel comfortable in their presence.'

'How do you know?'

Duro shrugged. 'I just keep my eyes open.'

'Anyway, we're not here for politics or philosophy. You are a black woman, so like a good black woman, go and clean suite twenty-eight for an Arab sheik, as you have been ordered by your white boss. At least you're preparing the suite for a non-white person.'

'Ah, but the oil money makes people colour-blind, my sister,' Kehinde said over her shoulder as she left the room.

20   Just Another Black Woman

There was no answer when Kehinde knocked at the door. As there was no 'Do not disturb' sign on the door, she went into suite twenty-eight to turn the beds ready for the night. Humming tunelessly, she touched the quilted counterpane. Something moved. Jumping back, she cried, 'Oh, I'm so sorry! I thought there was no one in. I just wanted to turn the bedcover, but I'll come back.'

'Oh, that's all right,' came the low, rich voice of the Arab guest. His modulated accent was similar to that of an educated Hausa in Nigeria. He was wearing a long robe with a white headdress, as if he had dressed to go out, before deciding to take a little rest.

'I am sorry. I can come back,' repeated Kehinde.

'Oh, no, go on with your job,' said the Arab, climbing out of bed.

Kehinde did not like people watching her while she worked. But she did her best to ignore him. She flicked the bedcover here and there, drew the curtains, and peeped into the marble bathroom. Her hand was already on the doorknob, when she heard the rich voice again.

'You speak English very well.'

Kehinde wanted to say, 'So do you', but remembered where she was. The hotel itself was fifty per cent Arab-owned. As Mrs Okolo with her husband beside her, she would have been rude to the Arab, however rich he was, but now she was a woman alone, making beds for rich Arabs in an over-decorated hotel.

'Thank you. I have a degree in sociology,' Kehinde said stiffly,

127

not knowing what to expect from the announcement. The fact of the degree made her feel she was entitled to hold her head up, despite being a cleaner. She at last felt equal to Albert's second wife, Rike, which was perhaps why she had embarked on the degree course in the first place. She looked squarely at the rich Arab. His eyebrows were slightly raised, with something like amusement on his lips. Kehinde hated him for his arrogance. She felt helpless and exposed, standing at the door, waiting to be allowed to leave.

The Arab took his time before he spoke again, then he said: 'My wives will be here in a few days. We are Muslims. I can tell you are a Nigerian, and most Nigerians are Muslims. I would like you to teach them English.' He said this in the voice of someone accustomed to buying his way.

'Keep your cool,' Kehinde told herself. Her education and background had never brought her face-to-face with an Arab before, though she had grown up in a neighbourhood with many Muslims when she lived with her Aunty in Macaullum Street. They had sold meat and hides, prayed several times a day and given alms to beggars. The Ebute Metta Muslims carried water in kettles with them, so they could wash and pray wherever they were, and they chewed kolanuts. They had not prepared her for this man in his silk robe, speaking in a low voice she found difficult to understand. His movements were so languid that Kehinde felt impelled to do something crude and violent. She attributed the impulse to her Taiwo, who never allowed her to accept humiliation. She wished she could refuse, if only to show this indolent man that she did not have to do as he said. Kehinde was sure that in his country he had an Egyptian or a Nigerian servant to open and close his lips for him whenever he wanted to utter a syllable.

But she could not afford to refuse. She badly needed money to send to Bimpe and Joshua, because their father had decided, in his middle years, to become a polygamist. Yes, she would teach the Arab's wives or concubines or mistresses, or whoever he cared to bring. She wanted to ask how long they would be staying

128

in this opulent suite, which was practically an apartment on its own.

'Yes, I will teach them English,' she said, with a counterfeited smile.

'Check them up this time tomorrow, Mrs . . .?'

'Kehinde!' 'Mrs' was not called for here. She waited for the sheikh to tell her his name, but he had already lost interest, distracted by a magazine on the coffee table. Kehinde looked round for a split second to make sure everything was done that she had come to do, when the low voice spoke again: 'Change the television channel, please.'

Kehinde looked pointedly at the remote control on the coffee table, and again restrained herself. She adjusted the television to the required channel and dashed almost blindly out of the suite before she was given another humiliating task.

Kehinde felt so low, she wanted to cry. Allah Baba! Albert had reduced her. Where were the dignity and pride in herself she had been taught at school? She was glad she had told the sheikh she was a graduate, even if it was only in sociology, a discipline which qualifies you for nothing. She did not allow the tears of frustration that were beginning to form in her eyes to fall onto her cheeks. Instead, she wiped her eyes vigorously, recalling Bimpe's letter: 'When are you sending for us mum?' Pride and self-pity would not send them money for the fare. Such emotions were luxuries she could no longer afford.

For some reason, she did not tell her new friend and co-worker, Duro, nor did she telephone Moriammo. She and Moriammo had become closer since the death of Tunde in a car accident a few months earlier. Moriammo was finding it difficult to cope since Tunde's demise. She complained that the house felt empty without Tunde, and took tenants in on the top floor, while she and the family kept the ground floor. Then she complained to Kehinde, 'I can't stand them. Why should husband and wife be dancing to records at eight o'clock in the evening as if dem dey throw party? After all, we all were married before, so what is their *shakara* for, enh? When I don fully recover, I am going to pick up my life and study for a degree, the way you did.' Twelve months later, she still had not started the degree. She did not even bother to go back to her old job after the funeral. 'After all, I no have no mortgage to pay any more,' she said. Kehinde did not feel it was appropriate to confide in Moriammo about the sheikh, so she kept it to herself.

In the event, only one of the sheikh's women arrived, and she could not have been more than fifteen. The sheikh was old enough to be her father. Kehinde could tell from her tired eyes and her sometimes awkward movements that this was a young girl being obliged to cope with frequent sexual demands. Kehinde was instructed to call her 'princess', while she was to address Kehinde by her first name.

'The others will be joining us in a few days,' the sheikh said, off-handedly. Kehinde was aware that he was watching the first lesson she gave the princess closely, even though he barely opened his eyes throughout. He reclined on the sofa and appeared to be asleep, but Kehinde knew he was listening.

She taught the princess how to say 'good morning' and 'goodbye' and how and when to say 'thank you'. Then she brought different objects and taught her their names, warming to the young girl's responsiveness. The hour passed surprisingly quickly, and Kehinde gathered her things and prepared to leave, with the princess waving goodbye, like the child she was. She was arrested at the door by the sheikh's languid voice. 'Wait, a labourer is worthy of his hire.'

'Labourer? Who me?' Kehinde thought.

The sheikh, without looking at her, took out an expensive leather wallet from his robe. Standing there with hooded eyelids, he flicked a handful of notes from a bundle of new bank notes, and put them on the table. Ignoring Kehinde, he turned and started to speak to his wife. Kehinde knew she was dismissed. The princess waved again and Kehinde left the room.

When she was in the hallway, she counted the bank notes in her hand and whistled softly. 'Not bad, not bad at all. What I earn in one hour teaching English is more than what I get for nine hours as a hotel chambermaid.'

The days that followed, she and the princess were left alone.

Kehinde used children's television programmes as a teaching aid, which provided them both with entertainment. As time passed, Kehinde noticed the other wives had still not arrived. One afternoon, the sheikh remained in his reclining position, reading a magazine, after Kehinde's arrival, though as usual he did not acknowledge her greetings or show any signs that he noticed her.

Fatima and Kehinde went on with their lesson. They were in one of the other rooms, and Kehinde's back was turned to the door when Fatima suddenly looked up, her face registering fear and surprise. The sheikh started talking to Kehinde in English.

'Your husband, what does he think of his wife working in a hotel?'

Kehinde turned so quickly that the counters she was using to teach Fatima fell off her knees.

'Many people work in hotels, so he does not . . .'

'Have you any husband at all?'

Kehinde stood up, holding her plump self as erect as she could. 'Of course I have a husband. He is in Nigeria at the moment, and I am doing this job to save enough money to bring my children over here.'

'Ah, children, children! That's what they all say.'

Then he turned to Fatima, and said something in Arabic. Whatever he said frightened Fatima so much that she hurried into the other room, covering her mouth to prevent her from crying out. In her haste, she trod on her black veil, and as it fell it revealed masses of beautiful auburn hair almost to her waist.

As abruptly as he had switched to Fatima, the sheikh turned to Kehinde and gestured with one hand: 'Take your clothes off! I want to see what a naked black woman looks like.'

Kehinde opened and closed her mouth, like a fish gasping for air.

'I don't want to sleep with you. I just want to see what you look like. I will pay you,' he drawled.

Sweat trickled from Kehinde's scalp down inside her dress. She was shaking like a leaf. She remembered the woman she had seen on the street when Albert was driving her to the clinic. How

131

long ago was that? She had called the woman a whore, but to fifteen-year old Fatima in the other room, she must have seemed like that woman. Fatima was the sheikh's young, innocent wife, bred for complete submission, but Kehinde was a black woman, cleaning hotel rooms.

'I say take your clothes off,' repeated the sheikh impatiently. 'I am not asking to sleep with you . . .'

Kehinde wanted to ask why he thought she would oblige, but then she remembered the international hotels in Lagos, where girls as young as fourteen swarmed around any foreigner, avid for foreign currency, and the hotel owners encouraged them in their trade, which brought in business. She picked up her coat from behind the door and walked quietly out of the suite. The sheikh might want to see what a black woman's body looked like, but that body was not going to be hers. She was aware that the man was speaking, but she ignored him, walking slowly down the padded corridor, past innumerable doors. She felt polluted and unable to go home. She needed the brisk, clean spring air in her lungs after the hot-house atmosphere of the sheikh's suite. Her feet led her out of the hotel, and she found herself on a bus going to Harley Street. She remembered that this was the street where she had passed judgement on another woman not so long ago. Now she wondered why the woman had been walking down Harley Street if she were a whore as Kehinde had called her. It had never been a red light district. Had she been looking for help? Was Kehinde's experience with the sheikh God's way of reminding her how women judge and condemn each other? She took the underground at Great Portland Street and arrived thoughtfully back at her house in Leyton.

At home, she took a bath, scrubbing herself so vigorously with her Nigerian fibre sponge that she felt raw all over. In bed, she tossed this way and that, wondering who to be angry with. With God, for creating her a woman? With men like the sheikh and Albert, who felt women should just acquiesce in any ridiculous plan they made? With other women, who in their ignorance pass judgement on their sisters? Whose fault was it?

Near morning, she fell into a fitful sleep, from which she was

132

woken by a hesitant knock. It was the Caribbean tenant. 'Good morning, Mrs Okolo. You're sleeping late, or aren't you going to work today?' he asked, poking his head in.

'I'm a little tired, I'm just taking a day off,' she lied. Then she remembered her manners and said, 'But thank you, Mr Gibson, for checking on me.'

'It's no problem at all. Have a nice rest then,' he said, and departed.

Kehinde telephoned Duro to say she thought she was overdoing it, working day and evening. She said she needed a break, and asked her to apologise to Mr Butterworth on her behalf. Duro was puzzled. She and Kehinde were not close enough for her to ask directly, 'But what's the matter with you? One minute you want to do extra work, the next you announce you're doing too much.'

Kehinde was grateful that Duro did not ask for an explanation. They had been in England long enough to acquire some of the native reticence about personal matters. Even when Kehinde phoned the office a few days later, to say that she would not be coming back, Duro did not ask what was wrong. Privacy was not without its advantages, reflected Kehinde, especially as she could not put words to what was going on in her head. Even Taiwo's voice did not intervene to help her. It was as if Kehinde was being forced to sort things out herself.

Cleaning jobs were not difficult to find, and Kehinde found another at her local Marks and Spencers. She was too old for their managerial training scheme. The young woman at the job centre where Kehinde registered listened sympathetically to her story, reminding her of Leah, the girl she had shared a room with at the clinic. Like Leah, Melissa was a good listener and much younger than she was. When their eyes met, Melissa's were moist. She gave her particulars of some part-time vacancies being advertised by the DHSS.

'This one is a part-time job, I know, but you do need a social science degree to qualify for it. Or you could go on with your cleaning and when you've saved enough to bring your children over, you could apply for better jobs,' she suggested. There was a pause, during which they both pondered the absurdity of her advice. Melissa went on to explain: 'I went to Berlin last year, and the cleaners in my hotel were Turkish women who had come to Berlin to make money. Some of them were professionals too, who planned to go back to their country when they could afford to practise their profession.'

'It's the same in my country,' said Kehinde. 'Pay is low and many people are over-qualified, so many of us came to the industrial world to make a living. My children love life in Nigeria, but they too would rather come here to work, and maybe go back when they're older. I too hope to go back some day. Meanwhile, I want to earn enough to give me the option of going or staying. It will partly depend on my children.'

'Let's face it, children belong to our husbands in a different, more distant way than they do to us. Our sense of responsibility is more immediate and closer.'

'Has education helped us at all?' Kehinde asked, despairingly.

'Oh yes, education is helping. If you hadn't got a degree, you wouldn't have been considered for this three-day a week job. There won't be much male competition there. Most men and younger people want full-time work. But it's not demeaning work. And you can be sure you won't be asked to take your clothes off.'

As Kehinde walked out of the office, she wished Melissa had not uttered that last sentence. She felt her experience with the sheikh was too humiliating to joke about. That was why she had not rushed to pour her heart out to Duro when it had happened. Though Melissa had been sympathetic, Kehinde felt her hurt had been trivialised.

For some days afterwards, Kehinde sank into the depths of depression. Michael Gibson kept asking her why she was not going back to work, but she could not tell him that she was busy taking stock of her life, reassessing her value. One afternoon she responded irritably to his enquiry. 'You sound like my gaoler, Mr Gibson.'

He laughed, his teeth gleaming. Kehinde looked at him, and

saw a black man of middle height, slightly fleshier than Albert, dressed in khaki coloured work clothes.

'My name is Michael,' was all he said. 'I've told you that several times.'

Kehinde knew his name was Michael but for a long time she had listlessly thought of him simply as the Caribbean man who lived upstairs.

'Going to work, no matter what it is, is better than sitting at home. Troubles multiply when you sit at home, you know,' he said gently.

'I've been promised a job at the DHSS,' Kehinde suddenly confided.

Michael Gibson sat down on a chair at the kitchen table. 'Now that's good,' he encouraged her. 'It's good and dependable work, the civil service. When are you starting? They tend to be very slow in making appointments.'

'I know,' Kehinde replied. 'I'm keeping on my Marks and Spencers job until the civil service is ready for me . . . I'll make you a cup of tea, Mr Gibson.'

'Thank you Mrs Okolo, but I really don't like tea much. I drink too much of it at work already. How about going out to eat Indian or Chinese?'

Kehinde looked at him closely, her mind working fast. She had stopped protesting that all her thoughts were hers alone, and started accepting Taiwo's voice as a permanent part of her consciousness. Ifeyinwa had said that she was the most unconventional woman she had ever met, walking out of her marriage simply because her husband had taken another wife. She argued that if every woman left for such a trivial reason, there would be few marriages left, but Ifeyinwa had not travelled out of the country of their birth. She didn't know what it was like to be taken by her husband to a doctor to abort an 'unwanted' baby. Nor would Ifeyinwa understand how she could go out to eat Indian or Chinese with a man who was not her husband or even Nigerian.

'I've never really eaten out much,' said Kehinde.

'Really, why is that?' he asked.

'We always entertain at home, invite people round, cook and talk.'

'Then this will be a new experience,' Gibson said with a chuckle.

They went, and Kehinde enjoyed herself. Apart from takeaway fish and chips and the Wimpy lunches of her bank days, she had not explored this aspect of London life at all. She had seen many dressed-up people going to eat in the hotel dining-room where she worked, but for some reason she had thought that sort of thing was for other people. She was learning. When she thanked Mr Gibson, who had insisted all evening on her calling him Michael, she stretched out her hand to be shaken.

He smiled his slow smile and said, 'Good night, Mrs Okolo.'

'Kehinde,' she said, a little embarrassed.

'I was waiting for that,' he said in his musical voice. Michael, like many Africans abroad, reverted to his own way of speaking when he felt comfortable enough.

Kehinde avoided Gibson for some time, her mind full of questions. Why was he not married? What would people say about her going out with a Caribbean man over five years her junior? Should she allow the acquaintance to grow into friendship? Taiwo answered her in characteristic fashion. 'So what if he is five years your junior? So what if your children notice the relationship when they return? After all, are you hurting anybody?'

21   The Rebel

'Why doesn't Mr Gibson move out of the house now I'm back, Mum?'

'Because he doesn't want to.'

'But I want him to. If you won't give him notice, I will.'

Joshua, recently arrived from Nigeria, was flexing his adolescent muscles. Kehinde looked at her son, and saw the gangling youth he had become. He felt he had the answer to the world's problems, having been to Africa, where young men were made to feel they owned heaven and earth.

Kehinde, meanwhile, still had her life to live. At forty-five, she would be old in an African compound situation, but in the west, she was just approaching her middle years. She was not heartless, just pragmatic. A man-child did not need to kill his parents to establish his manhood. In her house, whoever she wanted to stay, stayed.

'Mr Gibson is not in anybody's way, darling,' she said sweetly to Joshua.

'But this is my house, and I want him out.'

'It's not quite like that. This is *my* house, though it may be yours one day.'

She waited for him to object that he was his father's first son, and that women don't own houses, but instead, he muttered sullenly, 'They say he's a homosexual.'

'Who says? Just because he's not married? This is England, you know, people are not obliged to be married here. And even if he were, what harm is there in that?'

Joshua stuck out his lower lip. '*Shio*, shameful. People like him should be shot. They carry disease,' he spat.

'Joshua, anybody who is sexually active can get AIDS. Even you. It's something you'd better think about, since you're so grown up.' Kehinde sighed, and lifted one foot onto the sofa where she was sitting. It was more comfortable, and besides, it was her sofa. In fact, it was her living-room.

Joshua looked at her in amazement. He had expected her to be the ideal Ibusa village mother, but she lived in London, not the village. Then he said abruptly, 'I saw you in bed with him.'

'Oh, is that what this drama is all about? I'm sorry, we weren't sure it was you. You weren't meant to, believe me, but it's not a crime to love. Your dad has taken two other wives in Nigeria, and I'm not complaining. That's one of the beauties of polygamy, it gives you freedom. I'm still his wife, if I want to be, and I'm still your mother. It doesn't change anything.' Kehinde laughed, as Taiwo, the spirit of her rebellious sister, took over. 'You have girlfriends, don't you?' she asked. 'And why do you think your sister Bimpe didn't want to do a degree here in London? Because she wants to be with her boyfriend, Elijah. And if you had taken the trouble to knock, you would not have seen what you were not meant to see. You used to knock when your father was here.'

'Mama, can't you see? He's not a Nigerian or even an African. He's a West Indian and years younger than you. You look ridiculous.'

Oh God, he really believes the nonsense he is uttering, Kehinde thought. Did he expect her to alter her behaviour because of his arrival? She was wondering what to say next, when Joshua went on: 'Legally, all this is supposed to be mine. Dad said so several times, you heard him yourself. Why didn't you challenge him then?'

'I know what your father said, but where am I supposed to live? Let me tell you something. When your Dad and I started out, we didn't inherit any houses. We worked to pay for our education, miles away from anybody who cared for us. You're much luckier. You have a good education, and a British passport, so you can make choices we didn't have.'

'I thought you were supposed to live for your children,' said Joshua.

'I did, when you were young. My whole life was wound around your needs, but now you're a grown man! Mothers are people too, you know.'

Joshua frowned. He was trying to come to terms with a mother who was behaving very unlike the mother who had brought him up. It seemed to him that Kehinde was not only depriving him of his rights, but ducking her responsibilities as a wife and mother.

'But Ma, they said I should take the house and look after you. All mothers want their children to look after them,' he appealed.

'That's very noble,' laughed Kehinde. 'But I don't need looking after right now. I need you very much as a friend, just as I need your father, Mr Gibson, Bimpe and many others. I have a degree, and a job at the Department of Social Services. I'm enjoying meeting people and leading my own life.'

'So, now your life is full, you don't need your family any longer?' he pouted.

'Oh Joshua, of course I need you. I just don't have the energy to be the carrier of everybody's burdens any more. I sometimes need help too.'

'But what about Dad?'

'What about him?'

'This is his house too.'

'I didn't drive him out of the house. He left and started another family. He's free to return any time he wants.'

'Then why doesn't he come?'

'I don't know. Maybe he doesn't want to.'

'What does that mean? Honestly, Ma, I don't understand you any more. I don't.'

'Do we older people always have to justify our behaviour to you, simply because you're young? I'm sure he has his reasons for staying away from London.'

Joshua stared at his mother long and hard. He had boasted to his friends that his father had given him a house, a fact he had dangled in the face of his new girlfriend, Moya. Before he left

139

Lagos, Albert had said to him, 'We men must stick together, and look after our women. The house in London is yours. Make sure it goes under your name. Your mother loves you very much and would be happy to see you make your claim. Get in some tenants and send me money monthly.' It had made Joshua feel important, as if he had a responsibility. When Albert saw him off at Murtala Muhammed airport, he had been bold enough to pat his father on the back and assure him he had nothing to worry about. But the mother he had found in England was different from the one he remembered. She had gone by herself and got a degree, and survived without any of them. Joshua had not bargained for what that meant.

Eventually, unable to win the argument, he wrote to his father. Albert advised him to go to the Law Centre. There, they told him without much preamble that the house belonged to his parents, and if his mother did not wish to relinquish it, there was nothing he could do.

'Who is paying the mortgage now?' the lawyer asked.

'My mum,' Joshua replied, without thinking.

'Then you are wasting my time. You need to go and sort out your own life, rather than interfere in your mother's.'

This was a very hard truth for Joshua. He had a grant to study agriculture, a subject that had fascinated him when he got to Nigeria. He had hoped his mother would retire gracefully, giving him the run of the house. The grant and the money collected from the house rent would have made his life comfortable as a student. Even Moya did not react as he expected when he told her it was beginning to look as if his mother would not let go of the house. She responded, 'Well, it's her house.'

'But when I met you, I told you that I had a house and that we would live rent-free as students. Wasn't that why we became friends?'

'That was one of the attractions, yes. But it didn't work out that way. So what! You thought your mother would pack up and go . . . go where? It's not always good to be saddled with a house at our age. Houses need looking after, you know.'

Joshua thought that she was laughing at him. Nonetheless, he

140

was determined he would go and have it out with his mother once and for all.

A few days later, Joshua saw Kehinde and Mr Gibson together in the bedroom. He dashed blindly out of the house, determined to make his mother feel ashamed of her behaviour.

But now talking to her face to face, she seemed to be glorying in it. Enjoying shedding her duties. Most Igbo women liked taking on the whole family's burden, so that they would be needed. His mother no longer cared. How could you deal with a rebel who happened to be your mother?

Aloud he cried, 'Shio, so what kind of mother are you then?' He pushed his chair back noisily and stomped out. The slamming of the street door echoed round the ageing house. Eventually it died down.

Kehinde sighed. She added one more teaspoon of sugar to the tea she had just poured herself and stirred it absentmindedly, looking into space.

"Claiming my right does not make me less of a mother, not less of a woman. If anything it makes me more human," she murmured to her Taiwo.

At length she put the cup to her lips. She felt the sweet liquid running through her inside, warming every part.

'Now we are one,' the living Kehinde said to the spirit of her long dead Taiwo.

Glossary

abi   interrogative expression, meaning 'isn't it so?'

acada   slang for university educated person, derogatorily applied to women

adah   eldest daughter

agbada   voluminous robe, traditional to Yoruba areas, worn by men

akara   fried spicy balls made of a bean batter

aso-oke   traditional Yoruba heavy woven cloth

Baba   Father (Yoruba)

boubou   robe worn by women, especially in Senegal, cut wide so it slips off the shoulder

chi   an individual's personal god, according to Igbo belief. The chi of an ancestor may inhabit the body of a descendant.

ehulu   beads

Eko   Lagos

gburu   degrading jobs for women in England

gele   woman's head-tie

get belle   become pregnant

get k leg   become complicated

ibeji   twins (Yoruba)

iro and *buba*   wrapper and blouse, worn by Yoruba women

iwu akpu   grated boiled cassava, soaked in slightly salted cold water; a traditional Igbo dish

iyabeji   mother of twins (Yoruba)

kererem   a long time ago

kora   stringed musical instrument, originally of Wolof people of West Africa

143

lappa   traditional woman's costume, a length of cloth wrapped around the waist

make shakara   be boastful, puff yourself up

moyin-moyin   small bean loaf, steamed and usually containing flakes of dried fish, chopped boiled egg, etc.

na wa   it's trouble or it's big trouble

nne-eyime   twins' mother

oga   boss, chief (colloquial)

ojugo   asker of questions (Igbo)

onilu   professional drummer

otu-ogwu   cloth wound about the body under the armpits

oyinbo   white person

oyokoyo   beautiful, irresponsible young female

palava   discussion, issue, argument

pikin   child, children

play koto   fondle

sebi?   Yoruba word, equivalent of 'isn't it?'

shuku   woven basket

tanda   stay put

tiro   kohl

wahala   trouble

woli   prophet of a charismatic church

yamutu   dead

THE AFRICAN WRITERS SERIES

The book you have been reading is part of Heinemann's long-established series of African fiction. Details of some of the other titles available in this series are given below, but for a catalogue giving information on all the titles available in this series and in the Caribbean Writers Series write to:
Heinemann Educational Publishers, Halley Court, Jordan Hill, Oxford OX2 8EJ;
United States customers should write to:
Heinemann, 361 Hanover Street,
Portsmouth, NH 3801–3959, USA.

BUCHI EMECHETA
In The Ditch

A harrowing and humorous account of a young, lone, Nigerian mother's determination to carve a place for herself against the odds.

New Edition

Head Above Water

Buchi Emecheta's autobiography, spanning the transition from tribal childhood in the African bush to life in North London as an internationally admired author.

New Edition

Gwendolen

A tale of lost innocence and betrayal of trust. *'Miss Emecheta's prose has a shimmer of originality, of English being reinvented . . . Issues of survival lie inherent in her material and give her tales weight'* John Updike, *The New Yorker*

New Edition
(Not available from Heinemann in the US)

Second-Class Citizen

Adah's fervent desire to write is pitted against the dual forces of an egotistical and unfeeling husband and a largely indifferent white society.

New Edition
(Not available from Heinemann in the US)

Destination Biafra

Destination Biafra dramatises the painful birth of the republic of Biafra in the late 1960s.

New Edition

Joys of Motherhood

'. . . a graceful, touching, ironically titled tale that bears a plain feminist message' John Updike, *The New Yorker*

New Edition